SEW SORRY

SORRY

ARON BEAUREGARD

DANIEL J. VOLPE

ISBN: 9798485785536

Cover, Back, & Interior Art by Anton Rosovsky

Cover wrap design by Don Noble

Edited by Candace Nola

Special Thanks to Mort Stone for Additional
Revisions

Printed in the USA

Aron Beauregard Horror
Coventry, Rhode Island

WARNING:
This book contains scenes and subject matter
that are disgusting and disturbing, easily
offended people are not the intended audience

The characters and events contained within this
book are purely fictional.

JOIN MY MAGGOT MAILING LIST NOW
FOR EXCLUSIVE OFFERS AND UPDATES
BY EMAILING
AronBeauregardHorror@gmail.com

WWW.EVILEXAMINED.COM

DEDICATION

FOR DADDI BACE & NUT

PART I:
CHARITY'S CACKLE

BY ARON BEAUREGARD

WITHOUT CONSCIENCE

"Get the fuck away from me!" Sissy yelled, flicking the flaming filter of her cigarette into the chilly winter air.

The smoldering butt bounced off the greasy, shaking man outside her window. Embers exploded off of his forehead, momentarily illuminating the darkness that shrouded him. The pain on his face fueled by the bone-aching cold intertwined with the anger that stirred inside him. But he still wasn't ready to give up yet.

He placed both of his grubby palms together as calmly as he could, trying to convey his hardship. "Please, miss, we're so cold and hungry," he pleaded, gesturing to the downtrodden woman and young girl at his side.

His rotten toothless frown manifested under his tired eyes, begging with every speck of his being. The woman beside him was equally grimy and bundled up to excess. Several coats and tightly wound scarves masked her face, and the shivering girl was her miniature doppelgänger.

Sissy couldn't read their expressions, but their eyes.

Their eyes said it all.

The gnarly woman squeezed the child's palm tightly, while her other hand clenched a trembling sign scribbled on cardboard that read, 'HUNGRY AND COLD.'

Sissy immediately locked her doors and rolled up her window. Through the glass, she elevated up from her lap, a gray stun gun. She activated it and a jolting beam of blue electricity launched from each of the metallic points.

"Stay the fuck back, you freaks!" she screamed, her eyes widened with a stereotypical instinct. "You get what you earn," she continued under her breath.

She stared up at the traffic light as the vagrants continued to shiver in the trickle of snowflakes. They'd backed up but were still just a short distance from her car door. The traffic light felt like it had been red for an eternity. She strongly considered running it.

"C'mon," she urged it on, refusing to acknowledge the presence of the needy people in agony.

Finally, the light flipped to green, and she sped away, creating separation between herself and the sad strangers as quickly as possible.

"They always want you to fucking feel bad. It's not my fault you're all so lazy."

A little further down the road Sissy looked over at the sign that read 'PIERCE PARK.' She activated her turn signal and carefully made her way down the freshly plowed but still icy road. The winter elements were harsh and unforgiving, but also the perfect accomplice...

"I hate coming to this side of town. It gets worse every time. But it's always worth it," she chuckled to herself.

As her Mercedes-Maybach passed through the trees and deeper into the park, Sissy shrewdly scanned her surroundings. Eventually the road led to the parking lot of a deserted baseball field. Sissy pulled in slowly and eyed her prize. The creased skin around her mouth leveled out momentarily as she licked her cracked lips with anticipation.

2

Her pupils came to rest on the massive, metallic, orange box that was erected a few yards from the field's entrance. The glistening Michelin Cross-Climate snow tires slowed to a stop. Sissy's headlights illuminated the donation bin. A childish font that read, 'HELPING HEARTS,' was plastered across the side of it.

"Come to Momma," she whispered while slipping a pair of fingerless gloves over her liver-spotted hands.

She exited the vehicle and left it running. Her feet started to crush through the snow until they arrived at the back of the luxury sedan. Sissy popped the rear open and gazed down at the bags and bags of second-hand clothing that cluttered it. She sifted through until she found the compact step ladder and extracted it from the trunk before slamming it shut.

Sissy then power-walked over to the monstrous donation bin, while again, continuing to carefully scope out her surroundings. She wanted to ensure that there was no one in her dark circumference on that frigid night. She required total isolation.

The sound of an aggressive dog barking off in the distance echoed through the gloomy air. She gazed across the field at the mesh of fencing that encompassed it. She heard the hound in the distance excitedly rustling against the rusty structure.

"Damn strays. Every time," she whined turning back toward the bin. "They're taking over this city."

Sissy's vigor was surprising for a woman in her early fifties. She moved around without issue, guided by the hot shot of adrenaline piping through her system.

She felt alive.

The thoughts dancing in her mind of what goodies might possibly be waiting inside the donation bin were like a drug to her. It provided a heavenly surge that was as vital to her existence as water.

From time-to-time, she wondered why it felt so good. She didn't know. But of the handful, this addiction was surely the sexiest skeleton in her closet. It sat grinning at her; if it could've winked, it would've.

She placed the mini chrome ladder in front of the sliding pull-down door and tried to ensure that it stood as stable as possible, despite the inches of snowfall that layered the ground.

She exhaled and blew a wad of hot breath into her greedy palms. A smoky cloud warmed them momentarily as she whispered, "Once it gets cold, they fill 'em with gold."

She took a few cautious steps on the ladder and used the box's exterior to keep her balance. Once she got to the top, Sissy pulled down on the donation door handle. She peered inside at paydirt; the contributions intended for the homeless and browbeaten folk were plentiful.

"Oh, yes!" she screeched.

She continued to hold the spring-loaded door down with one arm while she extended the other through the tiny window. Her chilled fingers felt slightly numb, but still had enough feeling to sense when they engaged with the slick black plastic bag inside.

She pinched the bag and pulled with all her might; it was a heavy one. Thoughts of the plentiful bounty of vintage clothing raced through her mind. Her eagerness was almost animalistic as she tugged, trying to draw the mother lode closer to the opening.

"Come on! If you went in, then you can come out!"

Sissy realized that the amount of strength she was investing wasn't going to be enough. She took a deep breath, then violently jerked the lump of sorry garments toward her with everything she had.

The force of the movement caused Sissy's body position to shift, and in turn, the slick footing gave way. The ladder tipped over sideways, and gravity's cold-hearted nature took hold of her.

Her grip on the door slipped off the handle and the arm that remained dangling inside of the charity chest got wedged deep in the hinge.

The roller-bearing opening smashed down on Sissy's fragile forearm and elbow. The sudden weight of her entire body trying to pull her limb down with her spelled utter disaster.

The announcement quality audible *CRACK* of her shattered bone rang out. The gruesome *SNAP* nearly made her ears pop. The affected area of her skeletal structure had broken awkwardly; the white shards splintered, stabbing through her casing.

The hot blood steamed its way out of the gaping hole that, had anyone been able to see, would've offered an intimate window into Sissy's throbbing muscle and other typically hidden anatomy. The crimson cascaded with fury; leaking both into the bin and outward. The initial wave sprayed and drizzled all over Sissy's shock riddled frame.

The adrenaline surging through her core seemed to stymie the overwhelming pain at first, but the dreadful nature of the situation wasn't lost upon her. Her vocal cords let out a shriek that sounded like they were being simultaneously ground against a cheese grater; distorted wails of a hellish human harp.

She screamed and she screamed.

Then she screamed some more.

But Sissy had gotten the exact environment she'd hoped for upon entering the park; one of total seclusion. She gazed back at her ultramodern vehicle that sat, still running, just a stone's throw away.

It wouldn't help her now.

Her phone lay charging in the console - uselessly. Her heat poured out of the vents and wouldn't be felt. Her chariot awaited but she remained hanging helplessly.

Sissy bellowed out into the night until her throat went hoarse. As the minutes ticked away, her moans became nearly inaudible.

The adrenaline shot that was keeping her sane was starting to wear off. Behind that wave of disguise laid pain. Pain the likes of which Sissy had never endured. She knew her howls weren't going to make it stop. She had no choice but to act.

With her free arm, Sissy reached back up for the handle. Her icy fingers curled around the metal, and she tried to pull herself back up in hopes of dislodging her garbled extremity. As she elevated herself higher, the door began to slide downward. Immediately, she felt the horrific sensation of the rotating metal crush down on her exposed fragmented bone and mangled median nerve on the other side of it.

The tortured tissue forced her failure. Her fingers again slipped off the handle and her body dropped back down the few inches that she'd been able to hoist herself up. The result allowed the already cavernous tear to rip a little deeper and the bone to cry out a little softer than it had initially.

The pain was too intense for Sissy to consider her next move. The blood was beginning to crust all over her body; most of it had already congealed due to the frosty temperature. She was exhausted and starting to feel sleepy. She looked up at the blackness in the night sky and realized, in that moment, it looked blacker than ever before.

STRIPPED

Henry Finn twisted the dial to 13 and pulled down on the lock. It popped open and he latched onto his locker. He didn't want to open it, but he knew that he didn't have much of a choice, he was going to need his math book.

A sense of nausea came over him, but he suppressed it. There was no way to avoid what came next. He pulled the locker open slowly, as if a monster might jump out at any moment.

The familiar sound of paper falling down confronted him until the crinkled sheets laid against his slip-on sneakers. An exhale of angst escaped him. When he found the courage to look down, he saw the message scribbled in poor penmanship over a sheet of loose leaf: 'YOUR MOMMY CAN'T STEAL A HALLOWEEN COSTUME FOR YOU THIS YEAR!'

Another color copy of an image that had been plastered everywhere on the internet for the last eight months sat beside it. One that depicted Sissy frozen solid. She was an arctic bluish color, dangling dead with a ghoulish expression carved into her face. Dried blood clung crusted to her while her distorted arm remained wedged in a large donation bin. At the top of the paper, in black Sharpie marker, it read: 'I LOVE HANGING WITH HOMELESS HENRY'S MOM!'

"Ay! Homeless Henry! You still wearing them clothes your mom stole from the bums?" a voice boomed.

Henry turned around and was confronted by a face that he was never excited to see; Ron Thompson. His reddish nutty hair was slicked back, and his uncommonly freckle-free face depicted a deep sense of enjoyment.

"Whatever," Henry mumbled.

"What the fuck did you say to me, you little piece of shit?! I didn't hear you! Say it again!"

"I said, fuck you, Ron!"

Henry tried to sidestep his nemesis, but Ron wasn't about to let him get away with that shit. He grabbed Henry by the collar of his shirt and slammed him against the lockers. The other kids, cluttered around the perimeter of the hallway, suddenly took notice. They all promptly diverted their attention to the altercation.

"I heard a rumor about your scumbag mother. You wanna know what it is?"

Henry remained submissive to the abrasive tactics. It wasn't the first time he'd gone at him, so he remained silent and awaited Ron's abuse.

"I heard she stole the clothes off dead bodies in the graveyard to make your zombie costume last year! Is it true?"

Henry didn't make a peep.

"I said, is it true, faggot?!" he screamed, dragging him across the wall, and ripping down some of the school's dime-store Halloween décor in the process.

"You got real fucking quiet all of a sudden, must be the hard truth, I guess. Did I hit a nerve or something?" he continued, dragging Henry's lanky body back toward the open locker.

"Fuck, just gimmie a break, man," Henry pleaded.

"I'll take that as a yes," Ron laughed, ignoring his appeal.

"Hmm, I bet these aren't yours either," Ron said, looking Henry up and down.

Ron ripped off Henry's backpack and drove a fist laden with distorted knuckles into his abdomen. The oxygen hissed out of Henry's airhole, but before he could even gasp, a second blow had already landed. In his stunned state, all Henry could do was crumple to the ground and listen.

"Give me that fucking shirt, thief," Ron barked, pulling Henry's tee shirt from his lower back all the way over his head.

Henry's scrawny bare chest was exposed to the crowd of students who began to cackle with delight. He remained teary eyed and gasping for breath as Ron reached for his belt.

"Gonna need these too!"

He ripped the belt off of Henry's pants and quickly unbuttoned his jeans. In one fell swoop, Ron's meaty fingers grabbed the waistline of Henry's pants, as well as his boxers layered beneath.

"Your cunt mother liked to do this, didn't she?!"

Ron stepped on Henry's lower back and pulled the pants down his legs like an eager rapist. Henry's pale ass and hairy legs were unveiled for the bloodthirsty crowd of testosterone triggered teens that had gathered. The laughter only continued to grow in pitch.

Once Ron got his pants down to his ankles, he quickly pulled off Henry's Vans and the socks underneath. He didn't stop until he'd acquired every piece of clothing that Henry had put on that morning. Ron gathered them up and stood over Henry's naked, coughing frame flanked by his hysterical peers. The boys found it funny while most of the girls were more grossed out than amused.

"Now I'm gonna go donate these, rich boy. It's a good thing that crook of a mother you had is fucking dead. Maybe they'll actually get to who they're supposed to this time around."

As Henry began to regain his bearings, the giggles from the cruel onlookers roared. As he regained his footing more tears began to drain from his face. He tried to cover up his exposed penis and balls with his hands as best he could.

"Hey! What the hell is going on over there?!" an authoritative voice yelled.

In a fit of pure fright and humiliation, Henry snatched up his bookbag and used it to obstruct the view of his genitalia. Then he took off down the hall and headed for the side door.

CYCLE OF SHAME

Henry sat trembling with long baggy pants and a hooded sweater covering his head. The chill of the frigid autumn air that had molested his body the entire run home still hadn't left him. A feeling of worthlessness toyed with his mind.

His bedroom was a mess; it looked like an intentional one. His prized video game console sat cool and unused; a rarity when he was hanging out in his room.

A collection of horror and rock posters plastered the walls that surrounded him. The imagery captured enraged, terrified, and downtrodden expressions that ranged from classic cinema slashers to emo and death metal bands. They acted as the physical manifestation of all he held inside.

A knock at the door interrupted his quiet sobbing. Embarrassment bitch-slapped him across the cheek. "Fuck," he whispered. With the fresh stench of life-altering shame fermenting upon his icy flesh, he didn't want to see anyone, but he knew he couldn't stay hidden forever. He straightened up as best he could and wiped away the wells in his eyes.

"Come in," he finally moused dejectedly.

The door squeaked open slowly. His father's shaggy mustache and concerned eyes filled the growing crack.

"Hey, Henry... can I come in for a minute?" Mr. Finn asked somberly.

Henry nodded his skull slowly but remained cloaked in his hoodie.

Mr. Finn entered the room and closed the door carefully behind him. His body language was as awkward as could be, like he'd just walked in on his topless grandmother.

"Listen, son, the school called... I heard about what happened with the Thompson boy. I want you to know that I already talked to them. They're expelling him, no questions about it. With everything he's done to you in the past, I'm pissed it wasn't sooner. I've contacted a lawyer too; he's going to pay for this. But just know, when you're ready to go back, you won't have to worry about him."

"Ready to go back? You don't get it, do you?"

"What?"

"I'm not fucking going back! There is no going back! I'm done with this shit!"

"I'm sorry, I know you've got to be humiliated by what he did to you. But don't let it ruin your life. Pineview is one of the better schools, or the best we can get around here anyway... you'd be doing your future a disservice if you didn't return—"

"I have no future."

"Well, maybe I can give Tressmont a call then. Maybe a switch wouldn't be—"

"When I said I'm not going back, I didn't just mean to Pineview, I meant to school."

"Henry, please, I can't let you throw away your entire education. People will forget. It'd be a different school system, for Christ's sake."

"You don't know what it's like, Dad. I'm never going to live it down."

"Of course, you will, you don't think I got messed with in high school? Shit happens—"

"NO! I'm not talking about what happened today!"

"Then what?"

"What Mom did. It's like people think I'm responsible, and-and because we have money, it makes it even worse!"

"Listen, I was married to her," a lump began to form in Mr. Finn's throat. Barely able to hold back his tears, he continued, "She was better than that. I go to work every day, and everyone knows. No one says anything."

"That's one of the small differences between kids and adults. From what I've seen, they don't change too much really, their tactics just evolve. Instead of saying it to your face, they do it behind your back. They're whispering about Mom being a thief. They're talking shit about you and me. And just like in school, how *I'm* Homeless Henry, at work *you're* probably Handout Harry. I'm not stupid. I wish in discussing this that you approached me with the same respect for my intelligence that you always tote to your peers."

"So, you're just done. You're going to let *them* win?"

"I'm going to go to Uncle Tim's for the next week, maybe more. I need to get away from here. Everything around this place reminds me of her. It reminds me of what she left us with. I can still smell her crappy perfume. She always wore too much. And every time I smell it, I feel like puking. I fucking hate her."

"So, you think hanging out with her loser brother is going to help you?"

"I do. In fact, going to Uncle Tim's is the only thing that's kept me sane this whole time. And, Dad, I'm in a real fragile fucking spot right now. I need you to stop thinking about whatever goals you had for me and give me some space. I'm not threatening you, but I'm just letting you know, don't push me right now. I never ask you for anything..."

Mr. Finn returned to the door without saying a word. His posture projected his disappointment, but despite his internal fury with the circumstances, he remained idle.

He knew the ramifications of the incident had warped his son. Despite wanting to, he restrained himself from slamming the door on his way out.

THE SICKO

Henry pedaled down the dark one-way until his bike dragged to a halt in front of his Uncle Tim's house. The front of the property was unkept. The neighboring houses were far better maintained, but his place was separated enough that he didn't stick out too severely.

The duo of manically grinning jack-o'-lanterns flanked the porch, and a tired ghost that had seen better days indolently stared back at him. He looked up at the spookily lit entry as he hopped off the seat of his ten-speed and let the bike fall into an assortment of dead leaves that infested the lawn.

Henry trotted up the steps, gripping the straps of his backpack tightly. He peered through the glass window with the soiled drape behind it. He failed to find his Uncle Tim and decided to knock on the door.

He listened. Inside it sounded like the eerie soundtrack of a horror movie swirling in the background. The shrill sound effects rushed his ears as his Uncle Tim's gruff voice overlaid them.

"It's open," he growled.

Henry entered the dimly lit kitchen and closed the door behind him. He could see the path into the dark living room. The lights were out and the only source inside the darkness was the glow from the 14-inch tube TV sitting a few feet in front of Uncle Tim.

The flicker from the film illuminated the various animals forever imprinted in his home via the borderline obsessive taxidermy collection behind him. The VCR was laid out on the floor in front of the tube it was attached to. It was running and had a vacant box for a movie titled 'The Sicko' sitting on top of it.

"Get her... get her," Uncle Tim whispered, watching on, with his eyes stretched like a child on Saturday morning.

Before interrupting, Henry's eyes hit the screen. He was immediately captivated.

The maniac in the film had just picked up the top part of a lava lamp. The boiled, gooey insides flowed hypnotically and sizzled in his hand. He allowed the hot glass exterior to burn his flesh before asking, "How do you think your daughter will feel about this?"

He smashed the glass exterior into her skull with such force that the scalding contents had no choice but to vacate their home. As a wide gash left the woman's face parting and oozing a rosy runoff, the lava-like goop slimed its way over her mangled mug. The unnaturally colored turquoise liquid and lime lard-like sludge flooded, searing her beautiful face and the split meat in the newly opened carnal crack.

"WHAT WOULD YOUR DAUGHTER THINK ABOUT IT!" the man bellowed.

Henry still didn't feel like he should interrupt his Uncle Tim. The guy really got into his movies. Henry was equally infatuated. In fact, his Uncle Tim was the reason he'd begun watching. He remained enthralled and quietly took a spot on the loveseat beside his recliner.

Henry watched a rape scene begin to unfold that was nothing short of ghastly. It hadn't actually started but he had a sixth sense about these things. He could see where it was headed.

'The Sicko' (or at least, the deranged man onscreen who he presumed to be) began to pound on the woman's slimy, blistering face. Each unforgiving blow increased in force. He drove his elbow down gratuitously, until the poor woman teetered on unconsciousness.

Henry watched the woman's facial tissue continue to burn and bubble. The catastrophic impact of the fiery fluid was so appalling that he could nearly smell the cells cooking through the television screen.

The sick man on the TV tore through the woman's clothing next. With relative ease he peeled off each article. That part made Henry uncomfortable. The prior events of the day replayed in his brain. His life *was* a horror movie.

He then proceeded to gnaw on her exposed areola, attempting to come away with the nipple. The camera work was personal, making the disturbing details more intimate than most any gory film Henry had seen before.

The Sicko's stained, mustardy teeth ground against the rubbery tissue before tearing a sizable amount away from her breast. She moaned defeatedly while her jumbled face and haggard grimace leaked the contents of the lava-lamp and internal fluids from her body.

The man then spread her legs far apart and reached for her face. He took a scoop of the violence that canvased her cheeks and rubbed it on her hairy pussy. The blood and slime saturated the lower lips, like she had just given birth to an alien.

The man inserted himself in and out of her tremoring body. Each puny thrust had little if any impact on her. The man grunted but seemed to be more irritated than anything. After an uncomfortable period of time that seemed to push the boundaries of this 'art,' he removed his hard member from the slimy hole.

He looked to the side of him, annoyance penetrating the madness in his pupils. Something bothered him deeply and he was itching to get it off his chest.

"If I rub your clit, maybe that'll liven you up a bit!" he explained, lifting up the cheese grater off the floor beside him. "What will your daughter think then?!" he screamed.

The madman drove the jagged strip of steel into her vaginal area and began to scrape it side to side vigorously. More morbid moans of the dying evacuated the destroyed woman's esophagus as the sensitive meat mutated rapidly into a bloodier state of massacre. If the prior uncomfortably long diabolic antics of the single shot film weren't enough of a premonition, the viewer would soon learn, that he wasn't stopping anytime soon...

Sweat poured from the man's forehead as his eyes exploded with rage. Ten strokes over her hood and lips turned into twenty. Then fifty. Then a hundred. Each moment in the film was real time. There were no fast-cut edits that allowed for even the minutest reprieve. No rapid progression. The viewer felt each excruciating stroke against the sensitive region.

More raw flesh.

More blood.

More meat.

More depravity.

Tiny minced hunks of the stretchy lips became so lacerated that, before long, the outer and inner lips had no material remaining to distinguish them apart. They had just become one slick, dripping patch of garbled genitalia.

The camera zoomed in on the horrifying hole that looked like it was now covered in bloody baby food, then, suddenly, the VHS tape began to distort. The macabre murder scene was no more. The grainy picture failed momentarily before finally transitioning to the unified chuckles of a studio audience. The set of the show was from ages ago and portrayed a black family eating dinner together and sharing a few jokes.

"What? When did I do this?!" Uncle Tim yelled.

"That sucks, I was REALLY getting into that," Henry said.

"SHIT! That's one of my god damn favorites. Don't get me wrong, I love Good Times too, but, hell, that thing was one of a kind. Whelp, don't do drugs is the lesson, I suppose..."

"Never seen it before."

"Maybe some other time, I'm not in the right mood now.

Don't really feel like laughing," he said, turning off the TV.

He picked up a box of cigarettes beside him and a small black lighter that stood upward on the TV tray. He lit one and inhaled deeply.

"Why are you back?"

Henry hung his head in shame. He didn't want to explain the details. It was a lot to digest, and the misery-inducing thoughts of the ordeal were still simmering in his mind.

"I'd just rather be here. The other house reminds me too much of Mom. It's exhausting. I never asked for it."

"That kid's still fuckin' with you, huh?"

Henry nodded his head.

"Tell me what he did to you."

"He kicked my ass."

Uncle Tim studied him and analyzed his body language. He was still holding back.

"It was worse than that. That boys kicked the shit out of you plenty of times before. You weren't like this... you seem different..." He pulled in another massive drag of the tobacco and locked eyes with his nephew, "Like something's been taken from you."

Tears began to trickle down Henry's face, but still, he held it together.

"He... he stripped me... naked. In front of everyone at school. He said that the clothes I had weren't really mine. That Mom stole them for me."

Henry watched his Uncle Tim take another massive hit; the end of the cig blazed like a mini-wildfire. He could tell his Uncle Tim wasn't happy with the explanation.

"So, you came here for pity?"

Henry shook his head.

"Then why the fuck are you here?"

"For information."

"Information? That's only gonna get you so far in this world. That ain't gonna solve the 200-pound problem that continues to haunt you. Just 'cause he's bigger—"

"That isn't the only reason I came," Henry interjected.

22

"Okay. I'll humor you. Why *else* did you come?"

"For an alibi," Henry responded coldly.

It took a moment for the answer to twist his lips into the shape; it wasn't one he was accustomed to. But as the proud grin cropped up, Uncle Tim pressed the little that was left of his butt into the ashtray beside him.

THE FATHER
OF EVIL

Ron sat drinking a beer in his room when the door burst open. He looked into the dread inducing gaze that gleamed in his father's eyes as he closed in on him. Clyde Thompson harbored a look of hatred that would've been out of place in most families. But the Thompson's clearly weren't most families.

"You piece of shit. You really fuckin' did it this time!" he yelled.

"What?!" Ron yelped, spilling his Budweiser all over his lap. Ron expressed an emotion his peers seldom, if ever, saw him expel; fear.

"Kicked out?! They fuckin' kicked you outta school?! I had to work a damn miracle to get your simple ass into one of these fancy boy schools on my chicken-shit salary! And you blew it! Fuckin' retard!"

Clyde exploded in his direction, securing his massive dirty hand under his son's throat, and elevating him from the chair up. The cracks in the wall behind him that were there before he smashed into it explained that this wasn't the first time. Ron's athletic frame now expanded upon the prior impression.

"What the fuck do you care?" he managed to wheeze out, despite the chokehold being applied around his neck.

"You're worthless. You're never gonna be shit, boy. I wish I'd a been smart enough to pull out, but no, I got stuck with your dumbass!"

"Maybe you won't be. Maybe you'll come home one day, and I won't be here."

"Don't tease me. I been alive long enough to realize that dreams don't come true in this life. When are you gonna learn to stop fuckin' with me?"

Ron talked hard in front of his old man, but the truth was, he was petrified. The terror of his father's personal disgust left him shaking and unable to find a smartass comment to retort with. The smell of the liquor on his bad breath was the worst omen imaginable.

"You gonna learn, boy. One way or the other, you gonna learn..."

Clyde's greasy balding scalp thrust forward into Ron's eyebrow and the socket below. The stiffness of his skull caused a loud popping noise to fill the room. The blow left Ron dazed. He didn't even see the fist barreling into the same area until it had already cracked him.

The second strike left him woozy, and Clyde tossed him facedown onto the unmade bed beside them. He ripped at the waistband of his son's slightly oversize jeans until his ass was exposed. He watched the blood trickle out of his face and create a small pool on the unsanitary comforter he was sprawled out on.

"You gonna learn. One way or another, you gonna learn, boy," he repeated in a way that almost sounded like he needed to justify it.

Clyde picked what was left of the semi-cold beer off the dingy carpet and unbuckled his pants.

The warped man looked down with a look of imbalance festering in his eyes and toyed with his partially erect penis. He continued chugging what remained in the can, all the while, never taking his bloodshot eyes off Ron's asshole.

THE WRATH
FACTORY

When Ron awoke the next morning, he scanned the house slowly. With each step he took, his pulverized and torn rectum quivered in pain. Once the place was cleared, he felt a little better. But there was still one more thing he needed to check to feel safe.

He limped up to the front door and opened it, peering through the screen mesh outside. Clyde's rig was missing, and he was nowhere in sight. A wave of both sadness and relief crashed down on him. He knew if the truck was gone, he wouldn't return for at least a couple of days.

"Thank you," he whispered to no one in particular.

He wanted to break down and cry.

He wanted to let his emotions run wild.

But he wasn't the type.

Ron knew the things that were happening to him weren't right, but his brain was so muddled from ritualistic trauma that he just pushed it down. Like a gravedigger, he buried his eventual skeletons, bottling them up until they burst like his father had inside of his fecal cavity.

He needed someone to pass the pain onto. That was the only way he could deal with it. The task wasn't normally a difficult one, but now that he'd been expelled, it was definitely going to be more of a challenge than it had ever been before.

He looked toward the mailbox attached to the house and noticed it was overflowing with mail. Reaching inside he corralled the bundle before closing the door and locking it behind him.

Ron dropped the mail onto the kitchen table and staggered his way into the bathroom. He pulled at the toilet paper roll, collecting a large wad in his left hand before he dropped his drawers. He moistened the tissue with a little water from the sink and then spread his legs. Ron gingerly dotted his violated orifice and tried to wipe the dried combination of blood, cum, and crusted feces from the mashed-up sensitive hole.

With each wipe the pain pulsated through his system; a thud of darkness prodding his darkest thoughts. It pushed him further away from the wave of calm that had washed over him. There was a violent undertow that sought to pull him into the bowels of depravity.

He was so broken.

The humiliation he felt was the worst kind; lonesome shame. As he cleaned the painful anal wound, he shook with angst. He trembled with wrath. He hated that image in the filthy mirror in front of him. He fucking despised it.

The stained wipe dropped onto the tile floor and Ron rammed his head full speed into the looking glass. The first blow spider-webbed it and reopened the slice just below his forehead. The next shattered the reflective surface into dozens of pointy pieces.

He screamed at the top of his lungs while continuing to blast his face into the tan tiles he'd just uncovered. He stumbled backward, losing his balance slightly before finally holding his bearings.

As the blood gushed from his cranium, he turned to the shower and twisted the handle. He stripped down while using his hand to test the water. Once it was warm enough, Ron stepped inside and tried to stop thinking.

DARK
DISTRACTIONS

Ron felt slightly better once he was dressed and no longer bleeding. He still had a slight limp to his gait, but the sad reality was that his body had grown accustomed to both the physical and sexual punishment that he often received. His regularly scheduled abuse was over. For now...

It was time for a distraction.

It was time to forget.

It was time to transfer the suffering.

He felt hungry but couldn't eat. It was always this way. There was a different breed of hunger surging inside him. One that couldn't be subdued by a cheeseburger.

Instead of food, Ron decided that a beer and cigarette should suffice. He cracked open another Bud and lit up one of the cowboy killers that was laying forlorn on the counter. When Ron approached the table, he considered sitting, but then thought better of it. He didn't want any pain to remind him of the prior evening's decadence.

Seemingly unsure of what to do with himself, he looked down at the heap of mail momentarily. He never got anything, but seeing his name typed out on a purple envelope made him look twice at the irregularity. Interestingly, there was no return address or postage on the exterior of the item.

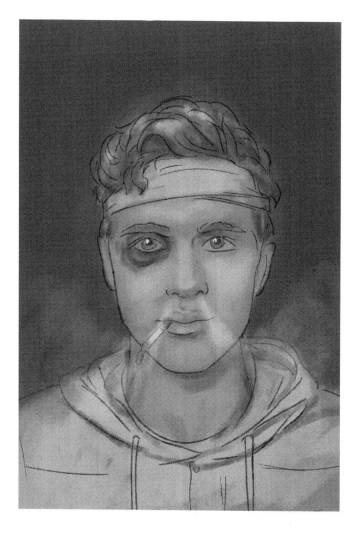

He set the beer on the table and furrowed his brow, stretching the tender skin under the bandage he'd just finished applying.

"Ouch, shit!" he moaned, pressing his hand gently against the afflicted area.

He took another deep drag of the smoke until the stinging pain subsided. The colorful envelope called to him again, so he refocused and lifted it off the table. Using his index finger, he burrowed under the packaging and tore it open.

When Ron lifted the single lone piece of parchment contained in the pouch out, a flurry of sparkling glitter slipped out along with it. He found himself confused but still both intrigued and amused. Emotions that didn't land in his soul often. Feelings he hadn't expected to digest on that particularly shitty morning.

He opened the folded sheet and another shower of glitter fell onto the table below; a few fragments landing in his Budweiser.

"Shit," he laughed, not too mad about it.

The letter read:

Ronald,

I couldn't call you because I'm shy. I hope the letter doesn't feel weird to you. I can't stop thinking about the last time you fucked me. The way you choked me until I passed out. It pushed me to the height of arousal. I know I haven't really talked to you since it happened... I'm just nervous. I wasn't expecting what happened that day, to happen at all, and for a while I wasn't sure how to feel about it. But now, more than ever, I want it again. No. I NEED it again.

Let's go back to the old Bentley house like last time. I'm so fucking wet for you. I just wanna get twisted and feel your hand around my throat and your cock between my lips. I lifted a few beers from the fridge in my dad's garage for us to sip on. It'll probably be enough to get us wasted, but if you could bring a bottle of something, that would be cool too.

I'll be chilling in the basement where we crashed last time. I'll bring some sleeping bags in case we decide to stay the night.

Amanda

With each further sentence that Ron read both his grin and erection hardened.

"I knew she liked it. Little fucking slut," he mumbled to himself. He snatched up the beer, sprinkled with girly glitter, and took a big swig. "She just can't get enough."

A juvenile fling was the perfect thing to take him away from the horrors that were still scraped into his cerebellum. In fact, as he gawked down at the paper in disbelief, he'd almost forgotten about it. Almost...

When he took a step toward the ashtray, he felt his displaced rectal tissue ache. The burn of his father searing his most tender flesh. And just like that, the cozy feeling that had somehow stoked up inside him was snuffed out. Just like that, the hot dose of hatred that he'd pushed down between his guts sliced its way back into his forefront.

He didn't notice, but he was grinding his teeth again. He didn't notice, but his grip was crushing the beer in his hand. But even when he did, Ron got no satisfaction in crumbling some tin. It couldn't feel the pain.

It was time to find someone that could.

THE BENTLEY HOUSE

When Ron pulled up to the Bentley house in his sputtering Bonneville, it was nearly sundown. He drove around back so his car wouldn't be seen from the seldom used road, just in case. The Bentley house didn't have any power, so all the lights were out. Ron usually kept a lantern and a few candles in the basement; sometimes he crashed there when his dad went off the rails.

Most of the kids in the area knew it was abandoned, but still didn't go there. It was creepy as shit, but it wasn't haunted. Stories of the paranormal had never circulated about the place. Just stories of Ron and the things he'd done to people inside. Those accounts of violence and wickedness were far scarier than any campfire tale his former classmates could conjure.

Ron exited his car with a bottle of Yukon Jack in hand. He walked through the vast cemetery of spent bottles and cardboard cases. The broken glass beneath his boots popped and cracked with each step he took toward the rusted bulkhead doors.

When he tugged on the handle, it squealed open; that was always where he chose to enter. All of the house's other potential points of entry remained locked down and boarded up.

He made his way down the steps, inadvertently clearing out some of the cobwebs along the way. The musty cellar was massive and still filled with an abundance of random junk. There was a main area with a staircase in the center that led upstairs, and two separate paths that led to doors for additional storage rooms. Ron looked away from the stairs. He preferred to remain subterranean where his nefarious activities would have the ultimate privacy.

Once Ron got close enough, he could see each of the routes that led to the respective rooms. He typically used the one to the right, but the crack beneath the door at the end of the left-hand path was glowing.

"Hmm," Ron mumbled taking a few steps in the direction of the light. "Manda?"

There was no response.

He continued forward before calling out a second time, "Hey, Manda, is that you?"

The faint pairing of distorted guitar and heavy drums could be heard in the distance. Annoyance primed his face and drew him to the threshold. He pushed the door open as he began to speak.

"Bitch, you better fuckin' answer me when I—"

As Ron pulled the knob toward him and pushed his way into the dimly lit room, something felt off. Before he could take in his surroundings properly, he felt a slight pressure against his shins. A twanging noise emanated throughout the room just as he noticed Henry's face. It was doing something that made him uncomfortable: smirking.

Before Ron even realized he'd walked into a tripwire, the sharp metallic blade, which moments ago ran parallel to the wall, had already sprung forward. The force of the chopping motion was on him in a flash. The hair-splitting quality of the steel that found its way into his lower extremities would surely change his life forever.

Ron's left foot that was planted ahead of his right was completely severed just above the ankle. The blade penetrated nearly the entire right leg, causing his fall forward to snap the remainder of the joined bone. When Ron landed on the filthy ground his lone remaining foot was only attached by a thin strip of crimson skin.

"My fuckin' legs! My fuckin' legs, man!" he cried, looking down at the riptide rush of red that was escaping the severed veins within the mess.

The shock gripped him firmly as he looked away from the bloodbath that had transitioned him to a ghostly complexion in a matter of seconds. He found himself viewing the familiar face of his perpetual victim; Henry Finn.

"What the... what the fuck did you do to me?" he whimpered, wiggling against the floor like he'd been punched in the chest.

Henry squatted down, getting closer to his face. The happiness in his expression had faded somewhat. The overload of disturbing imagery was like nothing he'd ever seen. For a moment, he wasn't sure what to do.

But deep inside, he knew.

Deep inside, the demons coached him. They cheered him on like no one else ever would. His brain was rattled but they were happy to reproduce the blueprint.

"Do you wanna live?" Henry inquired.

"Wh—What the f—fuck do you mean?" Ron replied.

"You can bleed out if you like. Let every sad drop drain from your body, and just end it here. But that's the best I can offer. *Or* I can stop the bleeding. What'll it be?"

Ron continued to writhe on the ground in agony, jumping in and out of consciousness. From the fragments of what he'd heard, Ron finally mustered the strength to blurt out, "Do—Don't let me die... please..."

"You're a brave son-of-a-bitch. I'll give you that," Henry said shaking his head.

"Brave but stupid," Henry explained as he moseyed over to the old couch a few yards away from him and bent over. He reached around it momentarily, then made his way back to Ron's quaking body.

ARON BEAUREGARD

Ron was so overwhelmed by the hideous, life-threatening injuries inflicted upon him; he didn't even hear Henry lighting up the blowtorch. His psyche was spiraling so deep into panic that he didn't initially see the blue flame beginning to char and blacken the nub that his foot had once been attached to. He was so overwhelmed by the evil he'd been confronted by that it took a few seconds before the scent of his own scorched flesh invading his nostrils struck him.

"H—Hey! What the fuck are you doing to me?!" he screamed, starting to claw at the concrete and drag himself away from his aggressor.

"You made your choice, now you're stuck with it," Henry replied with an absolute certainness.

He twisted the knob on the side of the torch and the triangular flame flickered first before vanishing entirely.

Reaching behind the couch again, Henry returned to face Ron with a black handgun this time. He pointed it at his target's upper body. Just as Ron turned his head and his terrified eyes peeled back, Henry pulled the trigger.

The result of the gun firing was far different than what Ron had expected. Instead of a bullet, an oblong, syringe-like cylinder with a needle at the tip pierced through Ron's sweater. It hung sandwiched between his shaken cells with a red feathery tip poking out of the rear.

Despite the absence of bullets in the gun, the immense fear inside Ron still hadn't been quelled. His heart raced just the same, pumping the blood out of his lower body rapidly. Like before, he felt incredibly dizzy, but somehow it had been amplified. As the fluid in the dart bled into Ron's body, he could fight the overpowering allure of slumber no longer.

THE TRANSFER OF TORMENT

When the groggy distortions began to fade, Ron wished they hadn't. He awoke wishing everything he recalled was anything but reality. However, his suspicions were only validated by the total absence of his feet, nude state, and the heavy shackles that propped up his aching shoulders and pinned his arms high above his head.

There was enough blood on the floor to justify a massacre, but he was grateful that the messy puddle of liquid didn't seem to be fresh any longer. A thick, cauterized layer of carnal crust now capped off each of his gnarly nubs. The ends looked distorted, like beyond-burnt mini-pizzas were stapled to the bottom of his legs.

The pain was still there, so Ron tried to douse his palate in saliva to aid him in crying out. There wasn't much fluid to be found in his dehydrated chamber. He coughed and moaned as he looked away from his freak show form, taking in the rest of the basement.

Henry stood in front of a small table that rested beside the moldy couch. It took Ron a moment to realize what he was working on exactly. His feet looked far different when they were detached from his body. The pair of purposeful pieces that he'd been robbed of rested on the dusty cellar surface.

One of his two trotters was just an oily, glistening display of meat, tendons, and bone. Like a doctor's anatomy model, the foot shined, absent of skin, right down to the filleted phalanges. The uneven sheet of the rubbery exterior that had once encapsulated the foot sat, sickeningly just a few inches away from it.

The screams poured out of Ron at the rate of a soda fountain with unlimited refills. While his throat leaked relentlessly, his petrified sights shifted just a short distance away from the gory display.

Henry stood, gloved and gagging, as he clamped down on the other foot in front of him. He grimaced while burrowing a blood-smeared hunting knife under the skin atop the other foot. He paused momentarily and twisted his head sideways to the bucket beside him. A wave of chunky vomit exploded from his mouth and plopped down into the dirty white receptacle.

After a few more heaves, Henry used his sleeve to wipe away the lumpy traces of barf from the corners of his mouth. He was still sputtering, but eventually refocused on the task at hand and came to grips again.

Holding the nasty steel, he turned to address the rambling screams coming from his traumatized adversary.

"I was wondering if you were gonna wake up," he said, digging his fingers under the flap of skin he'd created on Ron's foot.

He pulled backward with everything he had, expanding the tear and degloving the soft-tissue. He continued to widen the gap he'd created with the knife, both peeling the skin off Ron's foot and using the blade to disconnect any uncooperative tissue.

The gruesome process continued to the soundtrack of Ron's screams. From the top of the ankle, down to the heel, then to the arch, and finally to the toes. To complete the skinning, he held the nearly raw foot down with one hand and used the other to tear off the human rag from the toes.

The stomach-churning ripping noise resonated, bouncing off the cement walls that surrounded them. Intermingled with Ron's screams, it was the lullaby that led to the darkest nightmare of all.

Ron gawked at his bare feet; the term had new meaning now. Then he looked down at the crusty stumps that were singed to disgust and affixed to his legs. In between his screams, he belted out a question, "What did you do to me?!"

Henry had moved on to scraping the skin, trying to get it as clean as he possibly could. The knife pressed into the underbelly of the elastic exterior and harvested a 'man-made' jelly. As Henry watched the raspberry gunk accumulate across the blade, Ron's words caused him to pause. In Henry's mind, the hypocrisy behind his query was amusing.

"What did I do to you? What did I... do to *you*? Jesus Christ. The answer you're looking for is NOTHING. I did nothing to you; you did this to yourself!"

"Please, I need a—a fuckin' doctor! Maybe he can still reattach them! Maybe they can figure something... oh, fuck..." Ron moaned, seeming to give up at any potential happy ending, the more he thought about it.

"I'm afraid that's not gonna happen. I'm not like you, Ron. When I fuck with someone, I don't plan on getting caught. It takes a lot for me to fuck with someone, congrats on being my first and hopefully, my last. But the sad reality of this situation is, at this stage, it's you or me."

"Come on! You can't do this to me! I was just fuckin' around with you. You can't—you can't just fucking kill me over a joke!"

"It was more than that, it's more than just 'Homeless

Henry' and you know it."

"But it wasn't like this! It wasn't—"

"Why did you come here, Ron?"

"What?" Ron mumbled, with drool streaks and snot pouring from his salty face.

"Just what I asked. Think about it, what brought you into this rotten house?"

He continued to cry and whimper, failing to answer the question.

Henry set the jammy blade down on the table and set the patch of skin down to dry. He then dragged the other piece from the first foot in front of him.

"You don't remember?" he asked, lifting a large sewing needle from the table beside him. "Well, allow me to remind you," he offered, running the end of a thick spool of thread through the oval at the top of the girthy pin.

"This place, you've made it your home. For some people, it's been a house of hell, or so the rumors suggest. Like Amanda Snipe, she was always a sad, gothic sort of girl. But the sadness she projected always seemed superficial, like an act. She seemed to have a pretty decent life but still wanted people to think otherwise. Teenage rebellion if I've ever seen it."

Henry pierced the needle through the slippery skin, at the heel, on one side of the rip that separated the foot's exterior. He then carefully crossed the thread over and inserted it into the other side. He watched Ron's watery and petrified eyes with pleasure as he tightened the thread, joining the two halves with the first stitch.

"But after she crashed here with you, after what the rumor mill claimed you did to her, she was a different person. Suddenly, that tortured character that she was portraying at school wasn't just a role. Suddenly, somehow, she attained all the inspiration that she needed to become that shattered girl that she always aspired to be. You're here because of a rumor. If you hadn't done those things to her, if it wasn't real, you wouldn't be here."

"That—That bitch fuckin' wanted it man! C'mon, she came to me—"

"Right, Ron! They all wanted it! She wanted it! I wanted it! Everyone wanted it! You fucking tool."

"I swear on everything! I'm serious!"

"You know, when I was throwing up in that bucket a few minutes ago, I was really questioning if I made the right decision. If I'd just gone overboard and ruined my life. But rethinking it now, I feel fine. I'm smart enough to avoid the cops, and brave enough to save so many other would-be victims from your indiscriminating crosshairs. This had to happen."

Henry finished stitching up the rear side of the first sheet of skin. He snipped the excess thread with a small pair of scissors and tied a bulky knot at the end. Serenaded by Ron's continuous screams, he moved onto sealing up the gaping holes left in the toe area.

"You think my fuckin' life is perfect?! It's not! It's—It's more screwed up than you can imagine!"

"Well, we've got a little more time still tonight. Tell me about it. I'm all ears," Henry said, brandishing a wicked grin.

Ron continued to sob hysterically. The look of humiliation in his eyes weighed down his urgency.

"It's not so easy, is it? It was hard for me to tell my Uncle Tim what you did to me. I know the feeling. I'm glad I did though, I'm glad that someone in my life wanted to see me grow some balls."

Henry lifted his eyes from the stitching every so often to check on Ron. It appeared he'd moved on from trying to converse and instead closed his eyes. He began to whisper to himself. The madness was gnawing into his brain. The poor excuse for a prayer that he offered seemed to be to no one in particular. He wasn't surprised to see that he'd given up on God.

As Henry finished sewing up the toe holes, he reached for the skinned foot in front of him. He faced the toenails toward Ron as he quietly chanted to himself and reached for the needle-nose pliers with his free hand.

He opened the jaws of the tool and clamped them down on the still-attached nail of the big toe. Once the firmest pressure he could offer was applied, he yanked and twisted the ridged plate back and forth wildly. After some effort he was finally able to uproot the nasty nail. A sickening crack tore through the room as the nail came free. He held it up to the portable light beside him for inspection.

"A little banged up, but not too bad!" Henry exclaimed.

Ron's eyes came open and he saw the ghastly sight of his removed toenail in the dim lighting. A phantom limb feeling came over him. It was almost as if he could still feel the agony that would have been sent to his brain had the toenail been still attached to his frame.

"What the fuck is wrong with you?!" Ron bellowed.

"I was just fine before I met you buddy. So, I'm just gonna assume that's a rhetorical question."

Henry reached for the tube of superglue beside him and squeezed out a healthy amount onto the bloody underside of the toenail. Then he applied the glued side back to the hollowed-out foot pouch he'd created.

"There we go, looks pretty good to me. Just four more to go now," Henry said to himself.

"Henry, what the fuck are you doing?! I know I said fucked up things about your mom and—and that I treated you like shit, but do you really think this is what she would want?" Ron cried, doing his best to search for any hint of humanity left in Henry.

"DON'T TALK ABOUT MY FUCKING MOTHER! Do it again and you'll regret it..."

Ron returned to unleashing a myriad of sad moans and scared sniffles.

"You still don't get it?" he asked, a bit shocked, and held up the vacated skin with the freshly reattached toenail.

"My mom loved clothing. Especially weird vintage and custom shit. She loved it so much she died trying to get it. She'd probably kill for something like this. Well, she'd have to, really. But this isn't about her. I hate that fucking cunt. She left a stink on me that I'll never be able to scrub away. For the rest of my life, I'm guilty by association!" he screamed, slamming his free fist on the table.

Henry gathered his emotions. "This isn't about her, it's about me," he grumbled maniacally.

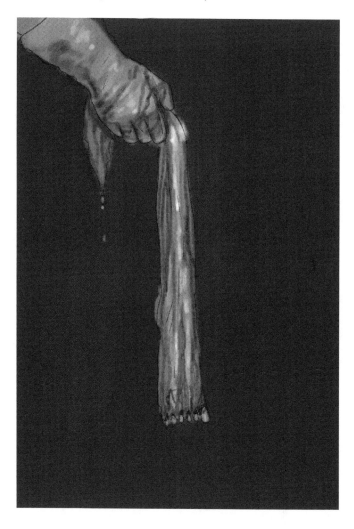

He composed himself once again, trying to remain calm. "That day at school, you took my shirt. You took my pants. You even took my socks... I've just about got one of the three back now," he laughed, flaunting the fleshy fashion he'd crafted.

"NOOOOOOO! NOOOOOOO!" Ron let out a wail that bordered on inhuman.

"Wait, calm down buddy. I didn't even tell you the best part yet," Henry said, really enjoying each new teardrop that Ron's eyelids set free. "In your honor, I'm going to donate the entire outfit!"

"You sick fuck!" Ron screeched.

"What can I say, you've changed me. I just feel like it's the right thing to do."

Henry reached for the dart gun on the table and readied it to fire. "But you're gonna need to get your rest. We've got a big day ahead of us tomorrow. It was tough enough making the socks, I know the shirt and pants are going to really be a chore."

"Please! Pleasssse! Help me! Somebody help me!"

"I'm doing you a favor. I could let you stay up all night with the pain. But then I wouldn't be able to keep you awake tomorrow. It's best you get some shuteye."

Henry fired the gun and the dart blasted into Ron's exposed chest. He watched Ron squirm and cry a bit longer before he finally screamed his way to sleep.

GRAVE
HATRED

Henry looked through the foggy gates of the cemetery as his bike came to a halt. He pushed it behind some of the privacy bushes that lined the morbid property and then hopped the spiky fence in front of him.

As his sneakers connected with the hallowed ground beyond the gate, he quietly walked down the rear path. It was farthest from the roadway and obstructed by tall tombs and trees that held what was left of their dead leaves.

The gloomy surroundings in conjunction with his purpose for being there left a strange and somber feeling stirring within him. The stress of the day's events and his internal anger battled beneath those.

When he saw the finely chiseled cross that stuck out of the private plot in the back, his heart began to thud feverishly in his torso. When the name "Sissy Finn" came into focus in the moonlight, the reaction of his organs only amped up further.

Henry approached the costly granite memorial, placing his hand over his cold face and resting it there for a moment. He wiped it downward, over his lips, preparing himself to articulate and funnel all that his brainwaves desired to vomit outward.

"This is all because of you. You made me. You abandoned me. You ruined me! And for what?! A pile of old rags?!"

Henry collected the runny snot that the frigid autumn air helped produce on the back of his tongue. Once enough of the chewy phlegm had been collected, he launched it forward. The greenish glob splatted against Sissy's smiling memorial picture that was imbedded into the stone and oozed down over her joyous expression.

"His blood is on your hands! You remember that! If you hadn't been such a greedy bitch, none of this would be happening!"

He rushed forward and rammed his shoulder into the stone, doing his best to try and knock the cross off of it. It moved slightly, but it would take much more effort to topple it. Henry's eyeballs flared with hate; he believed he had what it took.

The tears began to manifest in his eyes, "You turned me into a monster!" he roared.

He stood up on the small fencing behind the plot and pulled at the top of the cross with all he could muster. It drew backwards another half inch before Henry jumped off the fence while keeping his hands on top of the rock.

The momentum of the gravity, and his bodyweight, pulling down in unison, caused the religious symbol to tip over. As Henry rolled onto the grass a few yards away, the cross slammed down against the metal fencing behind it.

The granite was a superior rock that didn't crack upon connecting with the fencing, but when it tipped over the other side, it plunged into the soft ground and was left frozen in an upside-down state.

"A monster..." Henry whimpered.

While trying to restrain any additional tears for the woman that had betrayed him, Henry gazed upon the sacrilegious imagery he'd just created. While the blasphemous scene was unintentional, he couldn't help but think it was still appropriate.

GRUESOME
GUIDANCE

When Henry made his way into the kitchen, Uncle Tim was guiding a stream of Lucky Charms into a plastic Tupperware bowl on the table. He didn't look up at Henry, instead he continued manipulating the box, trying to get as many of the marshmallow bits to drop as he could.

Henry didn't say a word either. The look in his eyes said it all. He took a seat at the table and mindlessly stared forward at the wall.

"You want some dinner?" Uncle Tim finally asked.

"I don't think I can eat right now," Henry replied.

"Suit yourself."

Uncle Tim took his seat across from Henry and dumped an excessive amount of milk into the container.

"Did you text my father?"

"Yup. Took me a little while to remember how to use it again, but we've—I mean 'you've' been talking on and off all night."

"Good."

"What about you? Did you get to have a chat with your friend there?"

"We talked some. Whenever he wasn't screaming."

"That's good. Hopefully he understands the importance of all this before it's finished."

"I don't know why... maybe I just didn't think of it... but I didn't expect him to be screaming the whole time. It's like I can still hear him. Does that ever go away?"

"Well, during my endeavors, I can't say that any of them were alive long enough for me to encounter that. What you're doing is... it's really special. I'm proud of you."

Henry nodded his head, "But the screams that you did hear... did those ever go away?"

"Try not to think about it too much. After a while it'll stop bothering you. After a while, it's just like white noise. Just remember that he earned what you gave him. That always helped me through. But if it really keeps fucking with you, tape his mouth shut."

"I did that before I left, in case anyone was to pass by the house, but that's a good suggestion... that's a good suggestion..."

Henry's words trailed off in his mind. He was in a trance-like state. The last hours of extreme violence and sadism were all a nasty blot in his mind. One that he would be trying to figure out the outline of for the rest of his days.

"How much did you get done?"

"The socks are finished. Before I left, I started to make the incisions on his upper and lower body after he passed out. I should be able to finish tomorrow if I get in there early enough."

"Perfect, you shouldn't have to worry then. Sounds like he won't be making noise too much longer anyhow. So, I take it there were no issues with the spring trap and tranquilizer?"

Henry shook his head.

"And the techniques I showed you, those worked just

fine, I hope?"

Henry nodded in response.

Uncle Tim finally shoveled the first mouthful of his semi-soggy cereal into his mouth.

"I can tell it's wearing on you," he said after a couple of chews. "I know it's hard, but it gets easier. You're doing the right thing. Think about how many other people that cockroach would've fucked with. Whenever you're doubting yourself, remember all that boy's done."

"Yeah..." Henry managed.

"It'll be over tomorrow, and the world will be a better place because of it. But you need to get some sleep. You're gonna need it for tomorrow. You've gotta make sure that place is spotless. I don't want this ruining what comes next for you. But I wouldn't have let you do it if I didn't think you could handle it."

Henry's eyes glossed over again; the simple conversation was more emotional than he'd anticipated.

"What did my dad say?"

"He just asked if you wanted to go home, if you needed anything. Nothing special. Don't worry about him. I'll make sure he keeps his distance and that it seems like you were here the whole time."

While Henry watched his Uncle Tim inhale another spoonful of sugary goodness, he couldn't help but start to think about his mother and how he'd desecrated her final resting place. He discreetly let the tears absorb into the sleeve of his hoodie before looking up at his unflinching Uncle Tim again.

"Uncle, why do you think my mom was the way she was?"

Uncle Tim dropped the silverware into the container and let it rest. He took a deep breath and swallowed.

"The way that your mother and I got brought up ain't normal. We didn't have a pot to piss in or a working window to throw it out of. When she met your dad, it was like this whole new world was unveiled to her. A world that I've still yet to explore myself. Your father wined and dined her, showed her the good life. Once she saw that, there was no turning back."

"But if she had so much, why'd she still need to take from people that don't have shit?"

"The things we went through... they don't just all of a sudden disappear if you come into money. Like what that boy did to you, would any amount of money ever fix that?"

Henry listened with his head down and shook it once again.

"It was ingrained in her. It's ingrained in me too, to some extent. It's in our DNA. We lived our lives around some mean sons-of-bitches. We dealt with that every day. Either it was all that shit from the past... or it was just plain old selfishness."

"What happened to you?"

"I think that's a story for another day. But just remember, your mom was a fucked-up person. After what I saw done to her, if stealing donated clothing was the worst thing she ever did, they outta dig her ass up and saint her tonight."

"I just wish she didn't leave like that," Henry sobbed.

"HEY! Don't you fuckin' get soft on me! You came here to become a man! Men don't break down and start feeling sorry for themselves. I suggest you move past it now, otherwise, that shit'll consume you."

Henry straightened up and cut the emotional tirade short. He knew his Uncle Tim was right. He knew the man only wanted to harden him, to help mold him into something sturdy. A look of absolute seriousness crushed down on him. It wrung out every unnecessary sentiment and soppy thought that hampered him. Except for one...

"I just, I can't shake this one feeling."

"What's that?"

"Since the moment I watched the door open in the basement tonight I've felt it."

"Felt what?"

53

"Evil..."

"Well, sometimes, to defeat darkness, you've gotta spend some time in it."

SHIRTS AND SKINS

Ron was still incapacitated from the additional tranquilizers that Henry had shot him with when he returned to the basement that morning. He was groggy but awake until the new doses pulled him back down into the darkness.

Henry's expression was stoic as he squatted beside Ron's static body and continued working the blade under his pectoral muscle. The lacerations he'd dug in around his upper body before leaving the previous evening helped speed up the process. Most of the skin from his waist-line up to his shoulders was flopping loosely as he continued to separate the areas that remained.

The blood poured out, getting all over the set of gory clothing he'd left inside the room. As yesterday's crusty drippings married the current outburst, a disgusting texture caressed his body.

But he'd blocked it out of his mind; he was focused on

the task at hand. He saw the finish line ribbon, and it was comprised of an elasticized length of shredded, dripping tissue. Ron's tissue. It had been hours, but finally, the flak-jacket of flesh was ready to be ripped away.

Henry wrapped all ten of his fingers around the spliced matter and tugged it away from Ron's body. The slimy separation of the skin being yanked from the few areas it was still bound to was a nauseating noise. He leaned backwards, leveraging his body mass, while twisting and turning. The gag-worthy audio continued on, but as Henry tumbled away from Ron's atomically unmasked abdomen with the showpiece in hand, he felt nothing.

Despite the psychological soundtrack of Ron's screams from the prior night playing over and over in his skull, he moved past it in a very transactional manner. It was like a wolfish fiend had sought out his sensory veins and jammed them with a syringe full of Novocain. Pumping out the transformational contents throughout his fabric and sending a shock to his system.

Henry stared in a brief stupor at the otherworldly sight before him. It wasn't meant for the average person. ER doctors and surgeons who stared at perplexing text books and memorized tedious terminology were the only ones who were supposed to see this sort of bareness.

Ron's freakish figure remained footless, while his legs, privates, and waist being the next target area were littered with cuts. His mentally vacant face remained in place, but the mutilated missing torso membrane had uncovered his vermilion undertones. The sheen twinkled undeterred by the miserable lighting. Save for the splotches of subcutaneous fat that remained glued to some areas.

The lurid personal disclosure that Henry was witnessing was equivalent to tasting the forbidden. Suddenly, the fuzzy disorientation spawned by the numbness faded. He felt both privileged and dirty.

"Keep going," he mumbled, using the table a short distance away, to get his footing.

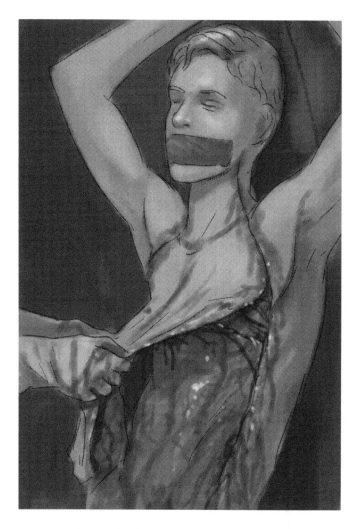

Henry knew that he probably had a few hours before Ron was pulled out of his slumber to the burning anguish that, beyond question, stretched the entire length of his upper body. If he was pulled out of his slumber at all...

With the type of damage Henry had just dished out, he wouldn't be surprised if Ron was already dead. As Henry readied his blade again and began to scrape the inner gunk off the fatty fragments of skin, he continued to watch him.

Ron's mini beer-gut inflated and deflated ever so slowly. It was slow, but still operable; he was somehow still breathing. Henry was comforted watching Ron's life support rhythm. He didn't want him to be dead yet. He didn't want him to miss out on the next demonic design that he had in mind.

Minutes turned to hours as he dried the horrific husk. Once it was reasonably dehydrated, Henry moved onto the next phase. He found the needle and stitching thread again and began to go to work. He tailored the terrifying top to the best of his ability, tightening the strings up the right side of the abdomen.

Once the shirt was bound together as a single leathery piece, Henry lifted up the scissors. He snipped the stitching at the various sew points and tied it off. But just as he was considering setting the shears back down, he thought better of it.

He repositioned the cutters and aligned the metal blades at the elbow of the left arm. He cut down into the stretchy texture, deciding to go with a short sleeve look at the last minute.

Once both of the forearm strips were laid out on the table, Henry took hold of one. A new idea carved its way into his broken mind. He cut a box shape from the patch that was about five inches on each side. He took hold of the rubbery rectangle and applied it to the front of the skin shirt.

Henry looked up at Ron's new ghastly shell and grinned. In that moment there was nowhere else that he wanted to be, then waiting in the darkness, becoming one with it.

It was just like his Uncle Tim had said.

He waited patiently for his sleeping beauty to awaken to a new horror. One that, as grim as it was, still wasn't quite finished yet.

SEW SORRY

Ron woke up screaming. While it wasn't a rude awakening that was completely foreign to him, it had never happened without his father nearby...

As appalling as those instances had been, this was somehow worse. The tape was an added layer that suffocated his expression, but it wasn't the added layers that were forcing the unheard vulgarities from his airhole. It was the subtracted ones.

His wet revealed muscles were cold. The agony stomped on every inch of his body. His vision was blurry, like a documentary film crew was streaming his sights. He could feel himself slipping away.

Henry stood just a few yards from his ravaged body holding up a finished article; a leathery bloodstained tee shirt comprised of Ron's casing.

"Thank God. I thought you were dead for a minute there. I would've been so fucking pissed," Henry said, exhaling a sigh of relief.

He pointed to the small patch of flesh from the forearm that he'd cut out and sewn over the right breastplate. "I even made a pocket. You could put your smokes in there or whatever really. And I found out despite us being two extremely different people, we actually do have a little bit in common!"

Henry moved around behind the table and set the skin sewn garment down. He let a lurid leer crop up on his face as each of his hands took hold of items in front of him.

Ron was still trying his best to shriek and yell the pain away, but the tape allowed little wiggle room. Despite his living hell, he was still engaged with all that Henry was showing him. He couldn't tell what was in his hands until he dramatically allowed them to ascend off the table.

"What are the fucking odds? We hate each other's guts, yet somehow, we have the *exact* same taste in our accessory choices."

As Henry's two hands came into Ron's line of vision, he saw a pair of relatively shabby-looking black wallets. They looked completely identical.

"Do you shop at T.J. Maxx too? I figured you would have more of a sense of style than me. I guess I was wrong though."

He set the wallet in his left hand down and picked up the fleshy shirt again. He angled the wallet and slid it directly into the flesh pocket he'd crafted.

"Look at that, *perfect* fucking fit. I mean, am I good or what? It's okay, no offense taken, I'm sure you'd applaud me if you could."

Henry's playful emotions seem to wipe away faster than water on a windshield as he set the casing on the table in exchange for the knife. He gripped the handle firmly and exhaled a deep breath.

"Now comes the hard part. It's gonna be tough for both of us, but there's no way around it. We can't let the needy soul that receives this walk around with their junk hanging out. No, the outfit is incomplete still."

Henry turned his attention to Ron and crept closer while swirling the knife around in his hand.

"No matter how you slice it, they're still gonna need pants."

Henry bent over and placed the tip of the knife under a hearty gash he'd left on Ron beforehand. Henry watched as Ron's disturbing hysterics continued; he flailed his butchered body like a man that had been set ablaze.

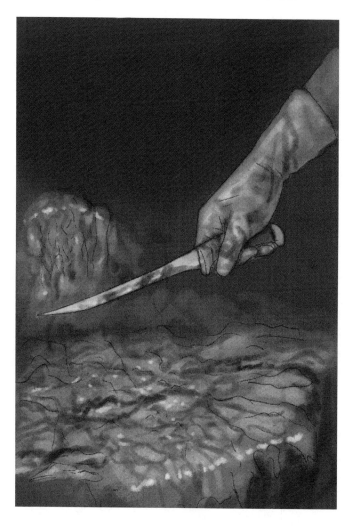

"Hey, whoa! Don't move too much, buddy. We don't want this thing slashing through a major artery or something."

Although Ron was thoroughly exhausted, that still didn't stop him from moving around a bit. Henry ended up improvising and using his knee to pin down one of his legs while he finished filleting his pelvic region as best he could.

"Relax. Just relax. Almost there, bud. We're almost there," Henry whispered.

Once he'd gone around the perimeter of his lower body and scrambled the blade around enough to dislodge most parts of the membrane, Henry set the blade aside and looked down at the floppy and sagging skin.

He looked back up at Ron, who continued to plead, stymied by the gray bar of adhesive that was placed across his lips. Henry paused, and after a brief moment of contemplation said, "Fuck it."

Henry stretched his hand to the corner of Ron's mouth and pinched the duct tape. Then, in one swift tug, he yanked all the layers away.

An avalanche of utter terror and remorse fell from the broken boy. Ron had seen the light; it wasn't far away.

"I DIDN'T—I DIDN'T MEAN TO—I—I'M SORRY! I'M SO SORRY! PLEASE! MAKE IT STOP! JUST FUCKING KILL ME! JUST—DO SOMETHING! ANYTHING!"

Ron's mad ramblings continued. They flowed non-stop as he searched as fast as he could for whatever combination of words might crack the code. But his hopes were dashed the moment Henry opened his mouth.

"Unfortunately, sorry's not good enough," Henry explained, while securing his grip on Ron's loose lower body shell.

"PLEASEHESSSE!" Ron wailed.

"You need to feel what it's like to be pantsed when you're not expecting it. But more importantly, we need to make sure one of those 'bums,' as you call them, is warm this winter. I know how much you care about them, and I'm sure your donation won't go unappreciated."

As Ron continued to beg for mercy, Henry pulled back, slipping the glossy trunks of torture down. The mangled tissue severed from Ron's frame, except this time Ron felt every molecule being maimed, every cell separating.

If the screams that haunted Henry previously were enough to keep his trauma tank full, these would cause it to overflow. The lower body skin slid down his waist, like a jock taking off sweatpants in a locker room, until it began to get hung up when it peeled down to his cock and scrotum.

Henry readjusted his grip, focusing on the pubic skin with both hands. As he ripped, and jerked the skin madly, it began to pull down further, an inch or so, with each tug.

Ron looked down at the monstrous display and watched helplessly as Henry brought the knife back into the equation. He burrowed the point with one hand and tugged down on the collective sheet of humanity with his other. Once Ron's skin had been cut and dragged down to reveal the literal redbone underneath, his consciousness faded entirely.

That didn't stop Henry from pulling the rest of the exterior off. When he finally worked it down to the bottom of Ron's desecrated body, he gave one final furious jerk. The result saw the skin slip from the nubs at the bottom of his legs and reopen the crusty caps that had been seared closed.

Plopping down on his ass, with the final piece to his evil outfit, Henry watched as a vile blend of pus, dark blood, and clear fluid rushed out from the re-aggravated raw stumps. Henry let out a deep breath of relief.

Part of him swallowed a great deal of the stress during the days of extreme exertion. He was thankful to know that the worst was over. The finishing touches that would tie together his malevolent ensemble were almost on the verge of completion.

ATTENTION TO
DETAIL

The revealing pieces of Ron remained in the untied black construction bag in front of the doorway in the cellar. As Henry's fatigued eyes gazed down at the raw muscle and bone, he couldn't help but still feel like Ron was there with him. If he haunted the house in life, surely, he would in death too.

Henry continued his thousand-yard stare into the gross collection. Every article of clothing he'd stripped from Ron's body (besides the ones he'd made out of it) sat squished on the side of the bag next to his parts. Then suddenly, it hit him.

"Fuck. The note," Henry grumbled.

The single item that, if found, could potentially lead authorities to the murder scene, he'd somehow overlooked. He'd accounted for every other detail of the operation, yet somehow, this important aspect had fallen through the cracks.

The scary part was, if he hadn't brought it with him, then Ron was too dead to explain where he might've left it. Was it at his house? Did he throw it away?

The countless scenarios overloaded Henry's panicking brain. Sweat beaded down the sides of his scalp while he listened to his heart thrash loudly as he eyed Ron's material pants.

"Fucking idiot!" Henry yelled, cursing himself for the situation he found himself in.

Henry leaned over and reached for the pants that Ron had come in wearing. He flipped them over nervously, and as he slipped his fingers into the first pocket, he extracted a mangled box of cigarettes and a lighter.

"C'mon, c'mon," he whined before going through a pair of empty back pockets.

He was starting to freak the fuck out inside as he turned the pants to the last pocket and held his breath. It was empty, all but for Ron's cell phone and a small keyring. It held the key to his car out back and a second that, he assumed, could only be the key to his house.

"ARE YOU FUCKING KIDDING ME!? SHIT!" he screamed, beginning to nervously pace around the small space.

"Okay," he let a deep pull of air release from his nostrils as calmly as he could. "Relax. Think. Maybe it's in the car!"

Henry raced out of the basement with the car keys in hand. He reached for the handle with his gloved hand and pulled it open. He searched the car carefully, trying not to leave any traces of himself inside the vehicle. He found nothing more than a collection of empty beer cans and crusty fast food.

"Okay, no big deal, no big deal. I know where he lives. I was going to leave the car on a random street, but—but maybe I can just drive it back discreetly and leave it there. I've got the key. I should be able to get inside pretty easily. It's probably out in plain sight. You can do this. You've come this far, this is nothing..." he lied to himself.

"Just take care of what I have to here, and then I'll get the fucking note," he mumbled, voice cracking at the thought of the stress.

He headed back down the steps and into the basement, recalling his mental checklist as he returned to the garbage bags. Henry was well aware that the clean-up had the potential to be the most monotonous and time-consuming aspect of his outline. He was right.

Just the blood alone was an incredible chore, but thankfully, had mostly been contained to the wall area. He understood that erasing any trace that people had recently been down there was the most important task he needed to complete.

After the countless hours of cleaning, and absorbing both wet and dried blood, Henry took some of the piled up, cobweb-clad stacks of garbage and filled nearly the whole room with it. He did his best to not interfere with the dust caked on the tops of the junk and bags, creating the appearance that they'd been sitting in those exact spots for ages.

He'd already removed the shackles from the area Ron had been held captive. He also detached the spring-loaded blade device from the wall, and tripwire used to trigger it. After those particular zones had been cleared, he made sure to occupy them with the highest heaps of the unwanted items.

He'd already cleaned and collected all of his tools and lumped them together in his backpack. Additionally, he'd bagged all of his own blood-soaked clothing and stuffed it inside, aiming to burn it at a later time. His goals felt like they'd been achieved. The room was nearly full now and looked like it hadn't been touched in years.

Overall, Henry felt confident that his meticulous attention to detail would keep him in the clear, should the authorities find out about Ron's dark times in the abandoned home. But there was one thing that still flicked his nerve endings.

Regardless of the cascade of cleaning and staging that had just washed through the room there was something that he couldn't account for. The potent aroma of the bleach was still strong enough to make Henry feel dizzy. The space had almost no ventilation aside from the small window at the rear of the room that he'd made sure to leave propped open.

He didn't expect that the world would drop everything and try to get justice, for a piece of shit like Ron Thompson, when the donation he was about to make turned up. He didn't imagine that the police force, who had a sheet on Ron that was like a roll of toilet paper, would be chomping at the bit. Henry just hoped that if, by some miracle, they did make their way down into the basement, the smell would have drifted away by that point.

However, if he was to savor the egotistical aspects of his sinister plot, the entire point of the sickening venture, he needed to ensure that he first collected the letter that lured Ron to the Bentley house. If that turned up, the cops would be all over the place and Henry's cover-up ability would be under severe scrutiny. He just needed enough time to keep them away while the stench faded. Securing the letter would ensure that happened.

"I'm smarter than him. I'm smarter than them," Henry said, attempting to build himself up.

Henry tied the plastic that contained Ron's body parts shut and tried to breathe in as few of the harsh elements in the air as possible. Then he quickly placed the plastic wrapped, skin-sewed outfit into a separate garbage bag beside Ron's dismembered corpse and sealed it up as well.

It was a good moment to grab a breather and take Ron outside. He could no longer be of any use to him now.

He dragged the hefty load down the cleared path and made his way back up the bulkhead stone steps. The fresh air felt good entering his lungs, clearing out the chemicals they'd been assaulted by. The evening sky out back was filled with an empty blackness that seemed all too appropriate for the task at hand.

Part of what made the uninhabited property so appealing to Ron was that it was far enough away from any other houses to avoid people getting wind of what might have been happening there. The 'NO TRESPASSING' signs kept most out, and the school rumors of Ron's menacing presence barred most anyone else.

"C'mon, you son-of-a-bitch," Henry huffed, dragging what remained of Ron into the tall weeds and family of trees out back.

He had dug the hole days ago, using one of the shovels that he'd found in the basement. He hollowed out the plot far enough back that there should be no earthly reason for anyone to stumble upon it.

Henry pushed the bag of beef into the cavernous pit in front of him and watched it plummet to the bottom. He then picked the shovel up that had been camouflaged by the weeds and, scoop by scoop, tossed the brown dirt on top of his evil secret.

After a few minutes, he'd covered the hole completely, and smoothed out the dirt on top of it. He gathered huge handfuls of the dead leaves that littered the entire area and dropped them on top, obstructing the visual below of recently turned soil.

Henry wanted to say a few words, something badass to cap off the two days of retribution, but all he could think about was getting that note. He could allow his arrogance to flourish when he donated Ron's rotten exterior. In his mind, it was no longer just about justice, it was about him.

He returned to the basement and hid the shovel behind more junk and then took his backpack with Ron's skin out of the room, closing the door behind him. Henry blended the items in with some clutter that was close to the bulkhead entrance. When he returned, he hoped to collect it and escape the grounds as quickly as possible.

Henry closed up the doors and raced to the side of Ron's Bonneville. The door opened, and he slumped down inside, as his mind was bombarded with thoughts about what came next.

He had no idea who Ron lived with inside his house or what it was like. Those were specific details that he hoped he wouldn't uncover during his infiltration. As he turned the key in the ignition, he heard police sirens wail off in the distance.

"One more fucking thing to worry about," he said putting the car in drive.

THE SCREAMS THAT NEVER END

At the budding age of sixteen-years-old, Henry was in the middle of Driver's Ed before he recently decided to follow the path of exile away from school itself. But that hadn't stopped him from learning how to drive on the low.

While his pulse thudded furiously, as his eyes searched for any sign of police presence, he recalled his first few times behind the wheel.

Uncle Tim didn't give a shit about him not having a license yet. From his perspective, if Henry was going to be a man, he needed to learn how to get behind the wheel as soon as possible. He knew his nephew was going to need all the help he could get when it came to both life and women. He didn't outright say it, but Henry knew it.

"Wheels'll make any pussy purr, kid. The faster you drive, the faster you'll be inside."

The line was one of many powerful nuggets of wisdom that Uncle Tim dropped on him. And like any good student,

Henry paid attention and followed directions.

But in that moment, as he rolled up on Ron's block, he knew that speed wasn't his friend. He brought the car to a crawl and killed the headlights. The street seemed dead, probably due to the late hour and the frigid weather.

When he approached the driveway this time, there weren't any cars parked. Also, another good omen was that the lights inside the house were off.

Henry looked around at the handful of generously spaced houses near Ron's and was grateful to observe them all seemingly occupied with other things than looking out their windows.

"Fuck it."

Henry slowly coasted into the dirt driveway and pulled the car up to about where he'd seen Ron leave it when he'd initially dropped the letter off.

The engine died as Henry extracted the key from the ignition. *Even better, if I leave it here and take the keys, they'll probably think someone picked him up,* he thought.

Staying low, Henry weaseled his way to the side door and inserted the only other key on the ring. He was sure it had to be for the house but was still relieved when he heard the lock pop open.

The smell of stale tobacco and spilled beer confronted him as he slipped inside. For all intents and purposes, he was satisfied with the state of the house. He didn't care how nasty it was, just that no one was inside it.

As Henry stalked his way through the dark kitchen, he almost couldn't believe his eyes. Right on top of the table sat the purple envelope with the sheet of paper inside it. The glitter that he'd stuffed inside for effect still sparkled in the lunar lighting that sliced through the curtains.

"Too fucking easy," Henry said, lifting the letter off the table.

But before he could celebrate, a massive pair of high beams lit up the windows in front of him. As the big rig pulling into the driveway let out a hiss, Henry ducked down.

"Fuck! Did he see me? Please, oh fuck!" he whimpered, while fumbling to fold the paper.

Mind gouged by the claws of terror, Henry folded the paper and slipped it inside his pants. The sound of a heavy door closing further prodded the fright flowing through every fiber in his body. Henry used his gloved hand to discreetly wipe the glitter off the table and let it fall to the filthy rug below.

He looked for other exits, but the door at the front of the house would do him no good if he wanted to avoid detection. *Windows,* his brain screamed.

"C'mon darling, right this way." The gruff male voice was right outside the door now.

As light-footed as he could possibly be, Henry tiptoed down the hallway. As he took in the horrifying sound of the side door opening, he passed a bathroom that had pieces of broken glass in the sink and all over the floor.

He continued down the hall to the end where there were two closed doors across from each other. Henry turned the handle attached to the one on his left, and just as the man's voice filled the kitchen behind him, he quietly closed the door.

"RON! WHERE THE FUCK ARE YOU BOY! I GOT A SURPRISE FOR YOU!" the voice yelled.

Henry looked around the room; it was a total nightmare. Rotten food, beer cans, and piles of filthy clothing were piled up everywhere. Pornographic photos of an extreme nature were plastered around like wallpaper. And there was a video shelf that looked to be overstocked with the most lurid material Henry had ever seen outside of the movies.

All of those things were gross and highly concerning, but not as concerning as what was mounted on every few feet of pink wall space on the edges of the bedroom.

There were whips, knives, ropes, choke chains, gags, and a full-sized sex swing dangling in the corner. Lastly, and most disturbingly, were dozens and dozens of diabolical dildos that ranged from modest to life-altering.

Some were smooth.

Some were massive.

Some were bumpy.

Some were metal.

Some were studded.

Some were knives.

The multi-colored cocks were all unique in their own way, but also shared something in common. Each had been used MANY times.

In the darkness, the fluids that stained them and the gnarly wickedness that had congealed to their surfaces, were not entirely discernible. But it didn't take more than those basic details to understand that something incredibly fucked up was happening in the room Henry currently stood inside of.

Henry scrambled, disturbed more than ever, looking for a place to hide. The lone window was blocked by the television screen and porno shelf.

"RON, GET THE FUCK OUT HERE! I DID THIS FOR YOU! I know I was a little hard on you the other day. Your daddy wants to make it up to you," he hollered as his heavy footsteps closed in on Henry.

Henry's shifting eyes finally came upon the sliding closet. It was cracked open a quarter of the way. As Henry positioned himself behind a mound of cushy clothing, he heard the door across the hall open.

"Ron—" there was a momentary pause in the man's thought process. "Where the fuck did you go? WHERE THE FUCK DID YOU GO!"

The ravenous outburst carried through the walls and into the closet with ease. Henry tried not to flinch, but the brutish pounding and pure rage caused his body to tremor slightly with each thunderous smash and roar. The sound of a fist blasting through the sheetrock wall sounded so close...

"You ran out on me, you fuckin' sissy! YOU DON'T RUN OUT ON ME! YOU DON'T RUN OUT ON ME, GOD DAMN YOU!"

A new softer noise joined the savage explosion in the hallway. It was faint at first but continued to become more prominent as the madness continued.

Henry's ears hated what they were being flooded with. The feminine crying sounded so innocent. A child's tone had no place near the demonic den he'd happened upon.

"Don't—Don't fuckin' cry! I wasn't yelling at you!" the man screamed. "It's okay, it's okay. We gonna go right to the bedroom over here, darling."

The voice seemed like it was moving further away, but moments later, it was right outside the door.

"I've got toys in here for you. Right in here, it's gonna be just fine, sweet pea," he said gently, deescalating his initially harsh tone.

When Henry heard the door close behind him, he thought he might be ill. Judging by the dialect of the crying youth, he knew her age must've fell in the single digits. His enemy's father seemed far more twisted than the worst rumor he'd heard about Ron.

Maybe this was why Ron was the way he was, Henry thought. That broken glimmer in his gaze, he knew it looked familiar. *He was holding back. Even when I was skinning him alive, he was holding back. That's how ashamed he was...*

Henry's mind flashed back, again he was bombarded by Ron's cries of agony. And the telling words: "You think my fuckin' life is perfect?! It's not! It's—It's more screwed up than you can imagine!"

He wasn't lying.

"PLEASE! NOOOOOO!"

The cry of the tortured child on the other side of the door shredded through his remembrance.

"It looks really scary, but it ain't so bad. I used to use it on my boy, he liked it some. But he left. You'd never leave me though, darling, would you?"

Henry wanted to put his fingers in his ears. He didn't want to hear the bedlam laced perversion unfolding on the other side of the closet. But he had no choice. If he blocked it out, Ron's father could open that door any minute. And there was no telling what he might do if he got his hands on him.

All Henry could do was hold back his tears and listen.

GREED OR GRIEF?

What's worse? The screams I created, or the ones I didn't stop?

It was the most difficult question that Henry had ever had to ask himself.

The screams, crying, and laughing in the bedroom felt like it had lasted for hours. Henry felt like he was coming unglued. It wasn't just the disgusting moans; it was also the disgusting noises.

The wetness.

The painful sound of forced insertion.

It had all gone quiet for some time now. Henry had no idea how long, but it felt long. The muffled orgasmic howls of horny women from the video playing in the background were the only thing that lingered on.

By his estimation it must have been at the very least forty-five minutes, if not more. He'd heard three separate scenes with different female vocals. Those scenes each had to be, at minimum, fifteen minutes.

Has it been long enough to test the waters?

He couldn't be sure if Ron's perverted father was still watching the nonstop spunk-fest. Ironically, as the thought processed in his brain, he was granted an answer.

The snore that cropped up was too guttural and congested for a young girl to emit. It was Ron's father, there was no doubt about it.

Henry knew he needed to make a move now, otherwise he may not get another opportunity. He did his best to push the vulgar and hideous details that he'd just audibly digested out of his mind. He wasn't thinking about anything else but getting the fuck out of there.

Each move he made past the piled, smelly laundry sounded like it was exiting a megaphone.

Still, the snoring continued.

When Henry approached the sliding door, he placed his hands gently on the wood and nudged it over just a little more to make space for himself. The squeaky sound of the seldom used tracks cried out.

Still the snoring continued.

When Henry elevated himself from the dark closet and his sleepy legs began to buckle, he took a wobbly step forward. He planted his heel firmly enough to avoid near disaster.

Still the snoring continued.

His instincts told him to get to the door immediately, but the direction that he ended up facing was right toward the bed in front of him. He couldn't help but freeze a moment and take in the repulsive sight.

Clyde's flabby naked frame laid with its eyes closed and sleeping on top of the comforter. His massive right arm sat outstretched, the weight of the obese limb pinning down the tiny body beside him.

But none of that bothered him as much as the widespread, bloodshot eyes that were staring back into his.

They were a pair of permanently ruined lenses. The heavy tears had continued pumping out of her pupils, long after the sadistic demon had fallen asleep. Henry had thought the screams had stopped, but they hadn't.

Her eyes screamed.

Her face screamed.

Her heart screamed.

His heart broke over and over as the sad girl's gaze burrowed into his sternum.

He wanted to help her, but he couldn't. The jeopardy he was barely treading water in was seconds away from sucking him down. One wasted instant could be the difference between obtaining everything or losing it all.

His psyche commanded him to leave but his feet somehow still remained in place...

FUCK! I can't just leave her here... with him, can I? I don't think I have a choice. The worst is over for her, maybe-maybe I can just phone in an anonymous complaint. Someone'll be over here first thing in the morning. Someone will save you soon, don't worry.

Henry would have given almost anything to talk to the girl and rescue her. *Almost* anything...

But he wouldn't have given his freedom. He wouldn't have squandered his chance for absolute vengeance.

As he turned his back, he heard a dim whimper exit the girl's dread addled body. A final and polite plea for her salvation.

Henry's heart cracked open further.

He wondered if she might scream. If she did, he couldn't blame her. The less selfish sliver of him hoped she did.

A tear ran down Henry's cheek as he cautiously turned the doorknob and exited the room.

THE FINAL
DONATION

During the fifteen-minute jog back to the Bentley house, Henry was forced to stop on several occasions because he was bawling so severely. He couldn't get the little girl's haunted, defiled expression or her scratchy adolescent screams out of his head.

"She didn't scream," he kept repeating to himself every so often.

Eventually, Henry finally returned to the dreary house, albeit not the same person that he was before he had left it. His jelly legs dejectedly jogged back down the cellar steps, nose still sobbing and discombobulated. He lifted both his bookbag and one that held his forthcoming donation.

When he returned to the trees on the back of the property, he approached another gigantic pile of leaves. This one was independent of the one that he'd layered over Ron's grave. He set the bags down on the side and reached into the mass of brown and orangey dead vegetation.

Henry was still trying to bottle his volatile emotions when he lifted up the handlebars of his bike out of the leaves and swung out the kickstand. He unsnapped the back storage case that was fixed to the rear of his two-wheeler and stuffed the sack that had Ron's shell inside of it.

He slung the backpack over his shoulders and jumped onto the seat as fast as he could. There was a burning urgency that was now boiling inside him. The longer the entire ordeal had dragged out, the more torturous it felt.

"It's time to finish this."

Henry stomped down on the pedal and sped out of the backyard and down the driveway. The freezing wind nipping at his skin made him think about Ron. How he'd never feel the bone-aching cold or sweat from a summer heat wave again. He wouldn't be dressing up for another Halloween, graduating (not that he would've anyway), or get hitched.

It's for the best. It's all for the best.

It was beginning to seem like Henry was trying to convince himself that the decisions he'd made over the past two days were the correct ones.

Did the evil and trauma inflicted upon Ron excuse the total cruelty he served up with regularity? Did his homicidal drive to stunt Ron's time on the planet in ultra-violent fashion and satisfy his own self-centered pilgrimage justify him turning his back on that girl?

He was afraid he knew the answers.

She didn't scream. She could've screamed. She could've told him that I was there. She didn't.

As Henry rolled down the slight hill and past the sign that read "PIERCE PARK," the guilt was devouring his guts. It felt like he'd swallowed a hot coal and it was burning a hole in his stomach lining.

Fuck Ron. All he did was hurt people. He would've never stopped if I didn't end it. This was the only conclusion.

Henry no longer truly believed his thoughts, but that didn't matter, he'd forced himself to accept that he did.

It was the only thing that made sense to do. He had no way of reversing it, so he may as well see himself in a just lighting.

As the spokes continued to tumble over one another, he realized that he'd finally run out of time to think about it. The bike rolled up to the same donation bin with the

"HELPING HEARTS" logo that his mother just couldn't resist.

It was the first time he'd been at the location of her demise. He wondered how she felt, hanging with her mangled arm and bursting liquid all over. Freezing to death in conditions far colder than the ones that were difficult in the fall. Did she think about him? Did she wish she could see him one last time?

It didn't matter.

All that mattered now was unloading Ron's shitty skin into the donation bin. Making his final stain one of morbid humor. How many jokes would they associate with his name? How many laughs would come at his expense? The possibilities were endless.

The bag at the rear of Henry's bike unzipped, and he extracted the oversized human shirt. He then collected the stitched-up shorts and sickening socks.

"Well, I guess this is goodbye, Rubber Ron," Henry laughed, looking at the sloppy suit.

The sound of dogs barking ravenously suddenly cropped up. He looked back into the fencing and trees, but the darkness of the evening left everything to the imagination.

He returned his stare back to the donation items.

"Rubber Ron, I like that. I think we can make that stick. In fact, I'll be the first one to make a meme."

Henry grabbed the handle on the sliding donation door and pulled it down.

"Until next time, douchebag."

The articles formed of skin didn't drop far. There were plenty of donations that already occupied the bin, and Henry heard them plop down on top of them.

Once Ron's remains had left his possession, it was like a weight had been lifted off his shoulders. Suddenly, all the horror felt worth it. The stress, and guilt, and hell that he'd harnessed in the center of his chest seemed to bleed out of him.

"I need a cigarette," he said with a relieved laugh.

He was semi-serious. He'd never had a cigarette, but figured if he ever got laid, he'd have one. Up until that last year, he'd never thought about killing anyone, but when the thoughts crept into his fractured mind, he figured if he did, that he'd have one.

The dogs that continued barking in the background were making him nervous. The area he was dwelling in was on the shittier side of town. The side that was flooded with imbecilic nomads. The side that had no problem selling cigarettes to kids.

As the dogs continued to growl in his direction, he decided that he needed to avoid attracting the wrong kind of attention. He'd just dumped about 20 pounds of skin in the metal box he was standing in front of. It was best he didn't stand in front of it for too long...

As Henry hopped on his bike he thought, *what fucking time is it anyway? Would a store even be open?*

It was hard to get a handle on things with Uncle Tim directing his text messages.

Even if a store is open, it's probably not the smartest idea to go inside. They might remember someone randomly popping in at an odd hour.

The gamut of creatively carved pumpkins that sat stoically on the porches further down the road was a nice treat for Henry. He loved the different designs and each eerie glow that he took in. He loved Halloween.

Henry continued down the main road, passing a group of bums.

"AY! Got any change, fucker?!" one of them yelled.

Henry ignored them and continued on. The side of town where Uncle Tim lived was a fucked-up place. But Henry's resentment for being born with a silver spoon in his mouth somehow made him gravitate toward the environment. Not enough to stop and engage, but enough to hang around.

There were still more masterful Halloween decorations being unveiled with each further pedal he pushed. Despite the appealing imagery that surrounded him, Henry couldn't overcome the dryness that was molesting his pallet. Killing had made him thirsty. He didn't know if that was normal, but he'd like to address it, considering the ride back to Uncle Tim's was at least twenty-five-minutes.

As he approached a closed Mobil gas station, Henry saw the answer. Outside, next to the car vacuum and air pressure hoses, sat a big radiant soda machine. The enticing flavors popped out from the backlit advertising.

PERFECT! NO CASHIER NEEDED! WHAT TIMING!

The bike rolled to a stop and Henry quickly extracted his wallet. He needed to move fast; he didn't know how many more of the vagrant leeches were circulating in the streets that night.

When he pulled the two flaps apart, he was surprised to see that there was no money inside.

"What the fuck?"

When he turned the wallet sideways to look at the ID card behind the laminated window, he realized that there was no ID card. To his shock and ultimate dismay, there was a license there instead. A license that read: Ron Thompson.

FAMILY TIES

As Henry raced back in the direction of Pierce Park, his calves throbbed and burned. He was no longer taking in the scenery, and he continued to ignore the vulgar weirdos who were at home in the streets. Nothing mattered, except getting back to that donation bin before anyone else did.

Fucking retard! You wanted to get cute and show him the pocket you made, and you put the wrong fucking wallet inside!

The idiocy was, without question, inexcusable. After trusting his preparation and blueprint, he'd overlooked the letter and now the wallet. How many other things had he missed?

There was no time to wonder, the window for correction was already closing. The joke would be on him if he wasn't able to get inside that fucking donation bin.

He arrived back on the scene to a quiet park. Even quieter than when he'd made his donation. He understood the irony of his situation, but he didn't have time to fuck around. He wasn't going to get caught like his mother, but he'd be caught by the police without question if they found his god damn wallet in Ron's breast pocket.

"Un-fucking-believable," Henry muttered.

When sizing up the donation bin, he immediately found himself wishing that he were taller. While the roller-bearing drop box could be opened if he stood plainly, to actually reach into the container he would need to be higher up.

He scanned his surroundings, looking for something to accommodate him. His bike was too awkward, the only other thing that was around was a steel trash barrel that sat just a few feet away.

Henry rushed to the trash receptacle and turned it on its side in front of the donation bin. The dogs started up again. They went fucking insane right when they heard the barrel tip over. Henry didn't have time to think about it. He jumped on the top of the steel barrel and quickly tested his balance.

It wasn't ideal but it was the best he had. He needed to get inside immediately, then exit the premises as swiftly as possible. Henry was hopeful it would be a quick lift. He knew from dropping Ron's skin off that the box sounded filled enough for him to skim it back off the top.

He pulled the handle down and cautiously peered in. He could only see the very top of the flesh tone skin peeking out over the variety of bags housed inside.

The door remained down as Henry's shaking free hand extended into the opening. He kept his balance as best he could. The barrel made it feel almost like he was surfing. That wasn't a good thing, considering the only wave he'd rode before went around the crowd at a baseball game.

Henry needed to reach in just a few inches further to have a shot at it. He elevated to his tippytoes as the trash can rocked back and forth. His digits tapped against the leathery exterior with a profound eagerness. But just as his fingernail snagged on the threading and tugged it toward him, Henry realized he was destined to repeat the error of his mother's ways.

His toes had overextended themselves and caused his footing to fly off the garbage drum. His body dropped full-speed and twisted awkwardly. As his fingers inadvertently loosened their grip on the handle, the arm Henry intended to snatch Ron's skin up with, dropped, wedging into the heartless hinge.

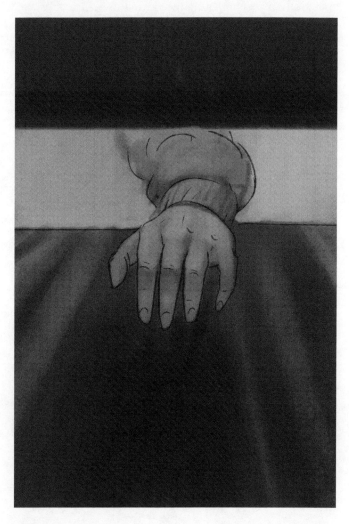

The door slammed shut with lightning speed. As Henry dangled, the screams that he'd watched pouring out of others with regularity, had finally come to possess him. He struggled to free his arm, but just ended up winding and hyperextending the joint even further.

His ligaments snapped.

His bicep tendon tore clean off the bone.

His forearm and humerus bone set off in opposite directions, deconstructing his elbow's outline entirely.

The popping and cracking of the bones left an internal distortion that looked like someone had cut his arm open, thrown up inside, and sewed it back shut.

Somehow, despite the violence unfolding at his joint, the carnage was still contained under his skin. Enough of the fragmented bone remained in place to push up against the exterior, but without penetrating it.

The gruesome distortion left him lightheaded and gripped by fright. But following the footsteps of the woman he'd come out of, Henry continued to fight.

He harnessed all of the fading strength he possessed, knowing if he didn't act now, he'd be done for. Amid the brutal screams he was trying to suppress, and wild growls of the dogs in the distance, his hand reached up for the handle.

His brains were scrambled, the emergency situation didn't allow him to properly foresee or calculate what might come as a result of his actions. Henry understood elevating his body was going to be painful, but he had no idea his simple effort would manufacture such intense agony.

The few inches he pulled himself up was enough to trigger ghastly catastrophe. Unseen to Henry, the hyper extended elbow joint pinned inside the roller-bearing had already partially collapsed in on itself. The subtle move added just enough pressure to the knotted limb for it to erupt in the opposite direction.

Without warning, the skin that, up to that point, had contained the internal calamity, gave way. The jagged shards inside blasted through his surface. A collection of muscle, tendon, vein, bone, and ligament pushed their way out behind a surge of blood.

Henry's arm had come undone, but there was still enough of his mashed essence wedged in the mechanism to leave him hanging.

"AHHHHHHHHHHH! HELP ME! HEEEELP! SO-SOMEBODY FUCKING HELP ME!"

Henry had found a way, but soon realized that he was barely able to yell. The torture he was enduring left him on the verge of blackout. The saliva leaking from his horrified yawn offered the same words that the baby in the bedroom's eyes had.

"She didn't scream. She didn't... scream," he managed.

Rude thoughts of a despondent future stabbed into his cranium. Crying for help would surely get him caught. It would leave him sitting in a prison, most-likely with one arm, getting fucked with until they stuffed his miserable ass in the ground.

Even darker thoughts began to enter him. What if he chose to linger? He would surely die soon without medical attention. Maybe he deserved to die. If he'd decided to help that child instead of obsessing over making a selfish spectacle out of Ron's destruction, he might not be dying a slow, throbbing death.

"She didn't scream."

Part of him now wished she had.

The choice seemed obvious. It was his time to drift away. While it was difficult to accept, he did a better job at containing his hysterics and outcries of anguish.

He was at peace with all but one thing. Legacy was something that mattered to Henry. Legacy was what had spawned the entire disastrous situation in the first place.

As his heart rate continued to pound, what felt like a parting thought came into focus. He couldn't help but imagine that, as sure as the stitching in his final donation remained tied together, so would the connection between Homeless Henry and Rubber Ron.

PART II:
THE STRAYS

BY DANIEL J. VOLPE

HUNGRY AND COLD

"Get the fuck away from me!" the woman sitting in the Mercedes yelled. She flicked a smoldering cigarette butt from the window, hitting Garrison in the forehead with it. The shower of embers illuminated the darkness of the cold, February night.

Garrison took a deep, calming breath, knowing if he yelled at this cunt, he'd get nothing. He shivered as a cold gust sliced through his threadbare and crusty clothing. As gently and non-threatening as possible, he put his hands together, as if in prayer.

"Please, miss," he turned up the beggar charm. "We're so cold and hungry," he said, gesturing back to a bundled-up woman and child.

Mary was wrapped in layers of mismatching jackets and scarves. She was tall but very thin. Her face was covered with cloth, only her eyes and a little of her nose visible. Desiree was equally wrapped up and was holding Mary's hand. In Mary's free hand was a sign that said, HUNGRY AND COLD.

Garrison hoped this little display of affection would do the trick and maybe get this stuck-up bitch to give him something. His hopes were dashed as she began rolling her window up and locking the door.

Garrison peered through the glass, trying to still get her attention.

She had an object in her hand and for a moment, he thought he was finally going to get something. An arch of blue-white electricity lit up her face inside the luxury vehicle. She held the grey stun gun in her hand. Her face was twisted in a sneer of disgust and anger, and her eyes widened.

"Stay the fuck back!" she yelled through the glass.

The next thing she said was low, too low for Garrison to hear, but he was able to read her lips.

'You get what you earn,' he was almost positive that's what she'd said.

He was a tempest. He wanted to smash the fucking window out and rip her from the car.

'Get what I earn? No, cunt, you'll get what you fucking earn!' he thought, his mind racing.

The snow began picking up as heavy wet flakes fell, but he could still see her, sitting there, almost willing the light to change.

Garrison took a step back, next to Mary and Desiree, as the big Mercedes took off through the light and then vanished.

"Fuck," he grumbled, as he watched the car turn the corner. He ran his tongue over his few rotting teeth, seeking the holes where some were missing. Garrison took a deep breath, feeling the rage build inside him. "Another hungry, fucking night," he said, turning to Mary and Desiree.

The woman and girl averted their eyes, not wanting to antagonize him anymore. They weren't challenging him, but he didn't need much to fly off the handle.

Garrison took a step towards them, his fists clenched. "You're both fucking worthless," he spat. "Fucking trash, the both of ya." He snatched the sign from Mary's hand. "Hey, dipshit, next time try and hold this up, rather than let it dangle." Garrison gave her a demonstration as if she didn't understand. "See, when it's up, people can fucking see it," he threw the sign at her face.

Desiree bent down to pick it up but didn't look at Garrison. She'd learned her lesson one too many times and didn't want to be hurt. The cold was painful enough.

"Go back to the fucking house and wait for me. I'm going to the park to check my snares." Garrison rubbed his face. His cheeks were numb, and the blowing snow made him squint. He didn't wait for them to answer; he knew they would listen to him. God help them if they didn't.

The walk to his hunting grounds wasn't too far, which was good. He was tired, cold, and hungry, and if there was nothing in the snares, he'd be pissed.

The wood line loomed in front of him. There was more than enough moonlight for Garrison to see by, even though the snow was still falling. The patch of woods wasn't much, but it was a perfect spot to catch stray cats.

Garrison stood on the edge of the tree line and listened. The sound of dogs barking in the distance caught his attention, but that was nothing new. The abandoned junkyard was home for mangy packs of dogs. They always fucking barked. He pushed the sound of the dogs from his mind and listened.

The wind howled and snow hissed, but something else caught his attention. In the distance, a cat whined and spat. It was music to Garrison's ears.

He crunched through the snow, his vigor renewed by the prospect of a meal. The woods were dark, but he knew where he was going.

The tabby hissed pulling against the wire snare. Its hind leg was a red mess; the wire biting deep into flesh and fur.

"Easy, now," Garrison said, creeping up to the scared animal. He pulled back as the cat swiped at him, barely missing his hand.

A collar dangled from the cat's neck. This was no stray, but a house cat, someone's dear pet.

Garrison smiled, his remaining black teeth reflecting the moonlight. A stray was great, but they didn't usually have a lot of meat offer. But a house cat? Now, there was a mighty fine meal indeed.

Garrison picked up a rock about the size of a grapefruit.

The cat, as if sensing what was about to happen, began to spin and twist. The wire cut deeper, ruining good meat, but Garrison didn't mind. There was plenty left, and he could wait to take his shot.

With its fur drenched in blood and the wire against the bone, the cat stopped fighting. It lay in the snow, which was dotted with crimson, and panted.

Garrison stood over the cat, looking into its fearful and exhausted eyes. He raised the rock and smashed the cat's head in. The rock made short work of the animal, popping its eyes from the sockets. The lower jaw was nearly detached, and a little pink tongue lolled from its mouth.

Garrison bent down and took the cat from the snare. He put the corpse in an oversized pocket of his jacket. The residual and fading body heat was nice, giving him a little reprieve from the cold. He stood and twisted to crack his back, when he spotted the headlights.

"What the fuck?" he muttered. The headlights were just visible through the trees and quite a distance away. "Now, who the hell is on the ball field at this time of night and what the fuck are they doing there?"

Garrison walked through the woods, his curiosity too much for him. Maybe it was a couple of teenagers fucking and he could get a quick show before robbing them.

He followed the trail through the woods until he popped out onto the snow-crusted baseball field.

A big SUV sat in front of the clothing donation bin, its HID headlights lighting it up.

Garrison saw something; actually, it was someone, hanging from the bin.

"What the fuck?" he muttered, crunching through the snow. He walked closer to the car, and it dawned on him, it was the woman from earlier. Absently, he reached up and touched the burn on his forehead from her cigarette butt. He winced...and smiled.

She was stuck in the bin. Good and fucking stuck. Her arm was wedged in tight and near-frozen blood dripped down the side. A small step ladder was toppled over near her feet.

Garrison crept over to her, wondering if she was dead. She wasn't, not yet anyway.

The woman's eyelids fluttered, but she didn't come to. Perfect.

Garrison opened her car door, relishing in the pure heat pumping from the vents. He jumped in the driver's seat, the ultra-plush leather hugging his dirty body. He put his hands up to the vents, willing feeling back into his flesh.

"Jack-fucking-pot," he said with a grin as he grabbed the woman's cell phone and purse. For a split second, he thought about stealing the car, but that would create a whole other set of issues. As badly as he wanted to, he didn't take the car. Garrison fished through her purse, plucking out her wallet. There wasn't much cash, about $100, but it was enough to get some food. The credit cards were useless to him, but he could sell them. He knew better than to use a stolen card, but there were some dumbasses who would. He kept digging, his fingers wrapping around a small, box-like item. It was a familiar one; the stun gun. He knew how to wake her up.

Garrison got out of the car, his body protesting the lack of heat, and walked back over to her.

The woman was moaning but wasn't awake.

Garrison put the stun gun in front of her face and arched it. Blue-white electricity jumped with a loud crackling sound. The result was instant.

The woman's eyes flew open, and she jumped at the sound. A new, fresh, hot wave of blood poured from her mangled arm. She yelled, which was more like a strained squeak, and stared at Garrison.

He held the stun gun inches from her face. The urge to plunge the prongs into her smooth, clean skin was almost painful. But Garrison wasn't a stupid man, not anymore. No, he wouldn't touch her, that would open an investigation. Rather, he'd let her hang, dying slowly in the cold and from blood loss.

"Remember me?" he asked, his rotten teeth on display.

She looked at him, the glint of realization and fear in her eyes. Quietly, she began to cry.

"Shh, shh, shh," he cooed. "Now, I'm not gonna hurt you, as much as I'd like to. No, I'm gonna let you hang here and fucking die." Garrison held up her purse, which was worth more than some cars, and said, "Remember, you get what you earn, and I've fucking earned this."

Garrison turned and left. The soft whimpering of the dying woman was like music to his ears.

BABY BIRD

Mary and Desiree sat in the small tarp shanty. It wasn't much, but it was home, at least for the time being. They didn't speak, rather just sat there wrapped in every scrap of clothing they owned. They shivered and Desiree tried to curl in on herself for warmth. There were a few Sternos left, but they knew better than to light one without Garrison being home. Besides, he was the only one with the lighter.

Desiree sat up and looked at Mary. She had a questioning look in her eyes, but still didn't speak.

Mary just shrugged. It was all she could do.

***

Garrison walked the streets, thankful there wasn't much traffic. The sidewalks were virtually untouched and covered in snow, so he stuck to the roadway instead. It was also a plus because there were no people out either.

Normally he wouldn't care, but with a jacket full of expensive goods and cat meat, he didn't want any confrontations. Still, he kept his hand on a relic of his past, his favorite tool and now favorite weapon; a sharpened cobbler's knife.

It was a Dexter Russell, one of his favorite brands. The blade was short, only about 4 inches, but it was sharp. For years he wielded that blade on various shoes and boots, now he kept it close by for protection.

Garrison put his head down, trying to deflect another arctic blast. Still, he pushed forward. The smoothness of the handle was reassuring, and the softness of the worn sheath was a comfort.

The wind stopped and Garrison looked up. He knew what he'd see even before he raised his eyes. His body was pulling him towards his past, something he could never escape.

A burned and boarded up storefront loomed in front of him. He slowly raised his eyes, knowing what he'd see, but felt the creeping apprehension.

The sign, charred and crooked, read 'GARRISON AND SON-Fine Upholstery and Shoe Repair'.

It wasn't the first time he'd passed his old shop and it wouldn't be the last, but something about this night made him stop. The wind blew, stinging his eyes. Tears welled up, partially from the weather, but mostly from ancient memories.

The shop was failing, but he never told Andrea. He kept up the facade, telling her and Tyler, everything was fine. That one day his 7-year-old son would have a shop to inherit. It was all bullshit. They weren't supposed to be there that night, the night the firebug came to help him with his insurance scam. The fire investigators said it looked like they had a party set up, burnt remnants of streamers and a cake. Andrea died with Tyler in her arms, their melted and charred skin joined together in death.

Garrison snapped out of his living nightmare, willing the sounds of their screams from his brain. He shivered, pulled his filthy coat closed and continued his trek.

The shanty came into view. It wasn't much, but it was home.

The city had many abandoned buildings. Most had been claimed by other homeless, but they were all filled with rats. He fucking hated rats, even their meat wasn't tasty, unlike cat. He chose to set up his little home on the outside of a building, rather than inside.

With a few errant sheets of plywood, sheet metal and some tarps, he constructed a shelter under an overhang of a building.

The shanty was dark and cold, as it should be. Mary had no way of lighting a fire and if she did, she fucking knew better than to light one without him. The only light was from a streetlight, which would keep the shelter lit, but dim.

Garrison grabbed the crooked door and opened it. He was right, no fire, just a cold woman and girl huddled together for warmth. The vision of Andrea and Tyler embraced in flame flashed in his mind. He willed the vision away and dug into his coat.

"Look what I got," he said, proudly displaying the cat. Garrison held it up by its hind legs, letting blood drip from the head wound.

Mary and Desiree looked at the dead cat like it was the finest feast they'd ever seen. Not eating anything besides snow for two days will do that to a person.

"No fucking thanks to you," he threw the cat at Mary. It struck her in the chest, a thin line of blood dotted her jacket. "Now, fucking dress this thing out so we can eat."

Mary grabbed the cat, leaving Desiree's side. The girl hugged herself, trying to retain some of the warmth she'd just lost.

Garrison wasn't going to give Mary a knife, no, she could use her bare hands.

Mary ripped at the cat's fur, trying to find purchase on the cooling skin. Finally, with numb fingers, she tore the animal's skin. She worked her grimy fingers between flesh and meat, until she could get a grip with both hands.

103

Mary pulled savagely, taking the moist hide off with a tearing sound. The cat was skinned and now it was time to remove the entrails. She tore a hole in the body cavity, opening it up.

The organs were packed tight, and Mary worked her hand up towards the cat's throat. She found the windpipe and tore. Blood oozed from the severed blood vessels, as she pulled the guts out in one fluid movement. Mary was careful where she put them; she had a feeling that would be the only meal her and Desiree would get.

"Give it here," Garrison snatched the skinned animal. He pulled his knife from his pocket and cut off a hunk of meat. "Get the Sterno," he told Desiree.

The girl slowly rose, not wanting to move, but knew she had to. She dug through the few items they had against the wall, plucking the metal can from the pile.

Garrison took it and rummaged through his pockets for his lighter. He felt the purse, his real meal ticket, and smiled. He lit the Sterno, relishing in the warmth of the chemical fire.

"Ah," he moaned, rubbing his hands over the toasty flame.

Garrison grabbed a stick and skewered the meat. He put it over the flame and listened as it crackled. Garrison loved cat meat, but his teeth, or lack-there-of, didn't. The few remaining teeth he had weren't strong enough to tear the tough flesh. That was where Desiree came in.

"Come here," Garrison gestured to the girl.

She was still wrapped up, her face covered with scarves, trying to keep warm. Desiree walked over to him, standing obedient.

"Take off the scarf," he ordered. Garrison dug in his pants and pulled out a small keyring.

Desiree unwrapped her scarf, exposing her face for the first time that night.

Her mouth was a nightmare. Thick, black stitches, which were normally used on boots, were woven through her lips.

They held the zipper in place. The zipper that sealed her mouth shut. On the end of the zipper was a small lock. The lock was secured to a metal hoop, which was pierced through her cheek.

Garrison took one of the keys and fit it into the lock. He removed it and placed it in his pocket.

Desiree relaxed as Garrison unzipped her mouth. Fresh air flooded into her lungs as she took a deep breath. She flexed her jaw, wincing at the pain in her tormented muscles.

"Thank you," she said, still not used to the zipper. Desiree never thought she could get used to it.

Garrison grumbled. "Well, it wasn't out of the kindness of my fucking heart, that's for sure." He took the charred piece of meat and handed it to her. "Chew it, but God help you if you swallow."

Desiree took the meat, nothing new for her, and popped it into her mouth. She didn't care for cat meat, but the explosion of grease and flavor was almost too much for her. Her jaw stung and an almost electric sensation shot through her at her first chew.

Garrison looked at Mary, who was still shrouded.

"Take it off," he told her, holding the key to her macabre zipper in his hand.

Mary unwrapped her face, revealing the same fate as Desiree. Her zipper was thick, and the stitches were crooked. She'd put up somewhat of a fight, but when Garrison stuck the tip of his knife against her vagina, she stopped fighting. *'You ever been fucked with a knife?'*

Garrison unlocked her mouth, taking the lock and sticking it next to Desiree's.

"That's enough," he told the girl. He crossed the small shelter and grabbed an unwashed plate. "Spit it here."

Like a baby bird feeding its young, Desiree spat the masticated lump of meat onto the plate. She ran her tongue around the inside of her mouth. Gently, she probed the zippers, seeking any bit of meat she could.

Garrison grabbed the pile of mush and shoved it into his

mouth. His gums and rotten teeth did just fine as he worked the meat around. Greedily, he swallowed. He picked up the carcass and cut another chunk.

The process continued until the meat was gone and bones picked clean. Neither Mary, nor Desiree had been given a single bite.

"Ah, now that was a great meal," Garrison said, rubbing his stomach. "You two can have the guts and pick whatever else off the bones. But you're not getting the Sterno," he recapped it, snuffing out the flame. "I'm going to bed." Garrison crawled into his filthy pile of blankets, wrapping a few of them around him. Within moments, he was asleep, his snores echoing off the thin walls.

Mary and Desiree looked at the pile of offal, which had since cooled. Quietly and somberly, they ate.

DEALS OF
FLESH AND BLOOD

Before long Winter faded, shifting into Spring. With it brought new life and warmth.

Garrison opened his eyes to dim sunlight working its way through the blue tarp. He yawned; the stench of his breath was offensive even to him.

Mary and Desiree slept on the other side of the shanty, each on a large piece of cardboard. Their mouths were unzipped, but that was so they didn't snore. Garrison couldn't stand snoring.

He rolled over and grabbed his tin mug. It wasn't much, but it was his favorite cup by far. He filled it from a bottle of water and put in 2 scoops of instant coffee. Garrison mixed it until most of the coffee was dissolved and drank it down. The jolt of caffeine worked wonders on an empty stomach.

Ever since that night, months earlier, things had been looking up for Garrison. The bitch's purse brought him in almost $500 and the credit cards sold for a pretty penny too. He was able to stock up on food and water, some of which he even shared with Mary and Desiree. Not for free, mind you, they had to earn their keep. There were no free rides on the Garrison train, which was for sure.

Mary had developed a knack for larceny, able to lift almost anything from a store. The fact she always had her face covered was a plus. She would steal, beg, or collect cans. Whatever she had to do to make money.

Desiree, on the other hand, had another set of skills. A set of skills that only a pre-pubescent girl could possess. She was in hot demand and Garrison was sure to get every penny he could from her.

Garrison swirled the last bit of his coffee and chewed the remaining grinds. He rinsed the cup, drinking that down too, and replaced it with his other meager belongings.

"Ok, get up," he said, trying to rouse the woman and girl. Neither of them stirred.

Mary grumbled, the metal of her zipper rubbing together with a grating sound.

Garrison's good mood was fading fast. "Hey, wake the fuck up!" he yelled.

Desiree's eyelids fluttered, but she still didn't wake. Neither did Mary, just another grumble, followed up with a wet fart.

Garrison had had it. "Get," he kicked Mary in the ribs, "the," his next kick was aimed at her face, which was wide awake and full of shock, "fuck up," his final kick hit Desiree in the small of her back. He was panting with rage as he stared at them reeling in pain.

Desiree reached behind her, trying to sooth the throbbing in her back.

Mary had taken the kick to her cheek and the damage was minimal. She tasted blood, but it wasn't a lot, thankfully.

"There, now are we fucking awake?" he spat, looking at both of them.

Mary and Desiree both nodded, still nursing their

wounds.

Garrison grabbed a chipped frying pan and a Sterno. He'd fashioned a small rack to rest the pan on, so he didn't have to hold it. Garrison emptied a large can of beef stew into the pan. He set it on the rack and lit the Sterno. Within seconds the shelter smelled like cheap meat and gravy, but to the three of them, it was heavenly.

Garrison grabbed a bowl from his stuff and filled it up. "Here, the rest is for you two."

Mary grabbed the pan and two bowls. She split the meager offering in half and handed a bowl to Desiree.

Desiree didn't even ask for a spoon, rather she began slurping up the food. Her stomach growled and cramped at the arrival of the meal.

Mary finished hers and wiped the sides of the bowl with her fingers, sucking the gelatinous gravy from her grimy digits.

Desiree licked hers clean, getting bits of mush stuck in her zipper. She didn't care. Her only thought was on getting as much food as possible. Her body was still developing and every day it seemed like she grew hungrier and hungrier. She'd been on the streets almost her entire life; well, at least since she was 7. She had no idea how old she currently was. It wasn't like there was a calendar on the wall. If she had to guess, she'd say 11, but that could be off by a year or two.

"Alright, let's finish up and get to work," Garrison said, his own bowl of stew almost done. He spooned the last drop of brown mush into his mouth. Even his rotted teeth didn't have an issue with the slop that came from the can.

Mary wiped her bowl, which still had a few crusty remnants of stew, with an old rag. She put it back with the others and stood up. She stretched and yawned, feeling the tension in her lower back. The ground, even with the cardboard, wasn't very forgiving.

"Where should I go?" Mary asked. Talking still felt weird with the zipper sewn into her face. She thought after almost a year and half, she'd be OK, but wasn't. She stuck her tongue out, touching the rough metal like it was an abscess in her mouth.

Garrison wiped his bowl out and put it back. He drank the rest of the bottle of water and looked at her.

"Well, stay off Broadway, that's for sure."

In a rare occurrence, Mary had been nearly caught. She was lifting some dried soup and chips, when she squeezed a little too hard. The bag burst and chips fell all over the floor. She took off before anyone had seen her, but she knew better than to test her luck again.

"Good idea," she replied.

"Yeah, I know," Garrison looked at her side-eyed. "How about the Flats? There's some decent stores on that side and they haven't seen you in a while."

Mary suppressed a groan. The Flats was on the other side of the city. It would take her at least an hour to walk there and then she'd have to start picking her spots or looking for an easy grab. Sometimes, if she was lucky enough, she could snatch a cell phone from someone's ear, but that was risky.

"I'll go with you," Desiree said. Her youthful face still retained a sense of beauty, even though she had a thick zipper on her mouth. "I don't mind the walk and I can help distract the clerks." She perked up at the thought of getting away from Garrison for the day.

"I can take her if—,"

"No, I have other plans for her," Garrison put his hand up, stopping the conversation right there. He rummaged through his stuff and pulled out a pack of baby wipes. "Here," he said, throwing them at Desiree. "Wash yourself, but mainly your little cunt and ass."

Desiree grabbed the wipes in shaking hands. She knew this was coming. It was too good of a money maker for Garrison. She fucking hated him for it. She hated him almost as much as she hated the men who used her. Her body wasn't ready for the trauma, it couldn't support a male frame on top of her. She tore every time and tried to cry, but the fucking zipper prevented that. Mary was no better. The older woman did nothing to stop it, even if she would only speak up.

"I'm going to take a piss. Both of you need to be ready when I come in," Garrison said, opening the door to the outside.

The alleyway where he'd built the shanty stunk like hell. Piles of old garbage, furniture and animal shit was everywhere. It didn't help the fact they used it as their primary bathroom. They would line an old spackle bucket with a grocery bag and shit right in there. The tied off bags would usually be hurled down the alley or sometimes taken to a municipal garbage can. It depended on how lazy they felt.

The building they were against hadn't seen a tenant in years and probably never would again. Garrison pulled his cock from his pants and unleashed a torrent of piss onto the side of the building. Cigarette butts and other debris floated along on his golden stream. He shook it off and dug in his pants pocket. He pulled out a pack of smokes, something he'd never done until he was on the streets. He popped one into his mouth and lit it with a match. The nicotine surged through his body, giving him a slight euphoric feeling. It was going to be a good day.

Garrison finished his cigarette and threw it in the puddle of piss. It sizzled and died, like so many before it. He opened the door to the shanty.

"Ok, are we ready for the day?" he smiled at them, with two locks in his hand.

***

Mary's scarf was light. It wasn't much of a scarf, rather a thin bandana. Actually, it was an old cloth napkin from an Italian restaurant. She had it tied loosely around her face, using a hair clip to secure it. Her hair, a dingy mess of brown, was down, partially obscuring her face.

The Flats were busy. A lot of foot traffic clogged the sidewalks, which was good. Mary was never much of a pickpocket, but if she had the opportunity, she might try. The stores were all busy, whether it was the pet store, the pizza places, pre-paid cell phone stores or pawn shops, they had customers. These were all great, but she knew what she was looking for; the pharmacy.

The pharmacy, it was one of the bigger chain stores, was a shop lifter's gold mine. Everything was expensive in there and it could all be resold for cash. The one item she was always on the hunt for was razor blades. For some damn reason they were a hot commodity on the streets. Probably because a pack of 2 cost damn near $20. Most of the smaller, mom and pop pharmacies, had begun locking their razors away. The big ones, they didn't care. It was a deductible loss, something else they could pass along to their customers.

Mary walked in, the scent of cheap perfume and makeup hitting her. She did her best to keep her head down, to avoid the cameras. Not that it would matter, most places didn't prosecute anyway. She was on a mission and moved with a purpose.

The racks of blades stood ready, and she grabbed a handful of the most expensive ones she could find. She hung back, watching the cashier, waiting for her moment to leave the store. Finally, it came.

The cashier turned to get a pack of cigarettes for a customer and Mary seized her opportunity. She walked out of the store, the sound of the security alarm silenced by the closing doors. She didn't run when she left, but blended into the crowd, trying to act natural. Mary kept moving, confident she'd made a clean break, when she felt a hand grab her arm.

She spun, ready to fight with a security guard, or just start crying. But it wasn't a security guard, it was Brian.

"That was a slick move, Miss Mary," Brian said to her, as he released her arm.

Mary tried to smile but forgot for just a second about the fucking zipper.

"Come on, let's chat," he led her to an alley. The alley, like many of the others in the city, was dirty, but Brian didn't live there. No, he was lucky enough to find an abandoned building that wasn't completely infested with rats and vermin. He even had a lock on his door.

His building was an old Chinese restaurant. The former owners, well actually the wife, decided to end their American dream with a classic murder/suicide. She shot her husband in the back of the head as he was having his morning tea in the front of the restaurant. She then put the gun in her mouth and decorated the ceiling with gore and bits of brain.

Brian was quick to move in, after the building failed to sell. He didn't mind the grisly history, in fact it helped to keep people away, which was a plus.

"Come on in," he said, opening the door for Mary.

She walked in. It didn't smell clean, but it was much better than the shithole she was living in, that was for sure.

Brian fished around in the gloom and found an extension cord. He plugged a lone lamp into the cord, lighting up the room.

The room was sparse. Brian kept everything in the back storeroom. There was no point in spreading throughout the restaurant. That would make it too easy for someone to spot him, so he stuck to the back room. A military style cot was against one wall. It was neatly made, albeit with less than military-standard blankets. A stack of old milk crates topped with plywood made a perfect coffee table. On the table was a small propane tank with a high burner on top of it.

Mary and Brian had known each other for just over two years. They'd both been panhandling by the interstate off ramp and struck up conversation. They gave their sob stories; she was an addict with a slight case of schizophrenia and no family, where he was a military vet suffering from PTSD, whose wife left while he was deployed. His wife's departure shouldn't have been a shock to him, but it was. She dug a little too deep and found things she couldn't live with. Brian had certain vices, a perversion which caused her to take their 10-year-old daughter and run.

Mary took her scarf off, the zipper reflecting in the lamp light.

"Oh, fuck that's right," Brian said, grabbing a paperclip from the make-shift table. "Ok, now stay still," he held the lock in his hand, careful not to pull against the ring buried in her flesh. "Almost," he said, wiggling the clip around, until finally it released with a click. He took the lock off. "There," he handed it to her, knowing it would have to go back on before she left.

Mary unzipped her face.

"Oh fuck, that's better," she nearly moaned. She moved her jaw side to side, relieving some of the built-up tension.

Brian lit the propane burner and got up to grab a pot. He filled it with water and set it on the flame. He sat on the cot and gestured for her to do the same. Not that there was anywhere else to sit, unless she sat on the floor.

The cot groaned under their weight but held firm.

Brian looked at her, examining the zipper/flesh patchwork of her face.

"Why do you stay?" he asked, looking over to see if the water was boiling yet. It wasn't.

Mary licked her lips, willing some saliva into her dry mouth. The zipper was rough on her tongue, and she could taste the leftover beef stew that was her breakfast. Her stomach rumbled at the thought of more food. She hoped Brian was planning to make something for lunch, but she wasn't hopeful.

She'd often asked herself that very question over and over. *Why do I stay?* It certainly wasn't out of friendship or caring. She didn't even like Desiree, in fact the girl was a burden. Before she came along, the food and money were only split two ways, even though it was never equal. It wasn't the luxurious living environment, that was for sure.

Well, why then? She knew why, and she didn't have to dig deep. It was fear. Pure, crystal clear, primal fear. Mary was terrified of Garrison, and he knew it. The things he'd done to her and the things he'd threatened, kept her in check. She thought about running away, but she knew he'd find her. She was his as much as the shoes on his feet.

"I can't," she muttered, looking at the pot, which was now boiling.

Brian followed her eyes and saw the water. He grabbed two mugs and dropped in a couple scoops of instant coffee.

Mary was disappointed, hoping maybe for a cup of soup or even broth. The coffee would do.

"Why not?" he handed her the steaming mug. Gently, he sipped his. "Just stay here and don't go back. You can run your racket here and I can put on my disabled vet act at the off ramp. Between the two of us, we can pull in some money."

"You don't understand, he'll find me," she sipped, burning her tongue. "And he'll fucking kill me." An idea struck her, a fantasy she had for a while. "Hey, what if we kill him?"

Brian was in mid-sip but managed not to spit his drink out.

"Yeah, let's fucking kill him in his sleep." Mary's eyes were alight with dreams of escape. "I'll let you in while he's sleeping and you stab him, or choke him, or whatever the fuck you want." Her smile was wide and full of metal teeth.

Brian was waiting for this. He had been ever since he first saw her all beat up. There was something he wanted, something to sweeten the pot.

"You want me to commit murder? And what do I get out of it?" he asked, a playful smirk on his face. He could fuck Mary whenever he wanted, but her pussy was old and beat up. It wasn't fun anymore and in reality, adult pussy never was.

Mary knew what he wanted, and she was more than willing to give it to him. "Desiree. We'll kill him, take whatever shit he has and take her. She'll probably come willingly, until she discovers...what you really are."

Brian put a finger to his chin as if in thought. Killing wasn't an issue. When he was in Iraq, he'd done plenty of it, some even with a knife. Sure, a few of them may have been surrendering, but fuck 'em.

"Don't leave me hanging. This will be the best baby pussy you've ever had," she tried to act sexy and alluring, but her body odor, breath and general unhealthiness was far from appealing.

Brian smiled at her and said, "When do you want it done?"

Mary could've jumped for joy. "How about tonight? No time like the present."

"Deal, but on one condition."

Mary would've given him ten conditions, but she was listening. "Ok, shoot."

He paused, thinking of how he was going to word his next statement. "Regarding Desiree," he began, "you don't try and stop me. From anything. Understand?" He was looking down his nose at her, like a teacher staring down a student.

Mary laughed. "That's it? Ha, I couldn't give two shits about that fucking brat. Garrison tricks her ass out all the time and I don't say a fucking word."

He grinned and raised his mug in a toast.

Mary clinked hers against his.

"Well, my dear, we have a deal."

***

The Imperial Motel was a dump. It was a classic, old-school motel, with chipped paint, a dried-up pool and pay-by-the-hour rooms.

Garrison led Desiree by the hand to a room on the second floor. It was supposed to be room number 10, but the sign had long fallen off. Since it was between 9 and 11, he figured it was the spot.

Desiree's heart was racing, and her hand felt sweaty in Garrison's. She always became nervous before a 'date'. She was scared, so scared. She knew it was going to hurt; it always did. More than the pain was just a sheer feeling of disgust. Desiree was only a kid, this shouldn't be her life, but it was. The time before her mother died, when they were first homeless, had been tough. After her mother died, the world took on a whole new shade of bleakness. Desiree was bounced around from family to family, each one promising to look out and protect her. Each one was a fucking lie.

They would beat her, abuse her, make her carry guns or drugs or do whatever they pleased. She ran from them all, promising herself she'd find people that actually cared for her. When she ended up with Mary and Garrison, she thought that was it. It was like having a mommy and a daddy, two people to look after her. Plus, there were no other kids, which was great. When there were other kids, things became complicated. They were usually mean and would hit and steal from her. No, Mary and Garrison were supposed to be different...but they weren't. Far from it. In fact, they were the worst and Desiree had nowhere to run.

Garrison knocked on the door. He could hear movement inside but took a second to prep Desiree.

"Now, this is just like the other dates, Ok. Nothing to it, just be a good girl and listen to him and you'll be fine." He tried to smile to reassure her, but honestly, he didn't give a fuck how she felt. She was doing it anyway, relaxed or terrified.

Desiree responded the only way she could; she nodded. Her zipper was covered by a scarf and locked up tight. She didn't know if Garrison would undo it for the date or not. She jumped as the door was pulled open, stopping on the end of the security chain.

A face peered out from the crack, a man with thick glasses, a fat face and a patchy beard. He looked at Desiree and smiled. His teeth were yellow, but not nearly as bad as Garrison's. He shut the door, undid the chain and re-opened it.

"Please, come on in," the man said, gesturing them into the room.

Garrison gave him a little smile and prodded Desiree into the room.

It wasn't much, but that was to be expected. Two full beds, a dated TV that looked like it was from 1996, and bathroom. That was it, no frills. The smell of a harsh chemical cleaner commingled with the deep-seeded odor of vomit, piss, semen and sweat. This room had stories to tell, and, in a few moments, it would have another.

"Take a seat," the man said, pointing to one of the beds.

Desiree knew this was for her. She looked at Garrison, who nodded at the mentioned bed. Slowly, she walked over and sat on the hard mattress. Even though it was firm, it felt like a cloud compared to the cardboard she was used to sleeping on.

"Here," the man opened a can of generic cola and handed it to her.

She looked at Garrison, hoping he'd unzip her mouth so she could drink it, but he didn't. Desiree held the warm can of soda, smelling the sugary goodness as the bubbles popped.

"So, $100 an hour, plus the room for 4 hours afterwards, right?" Garrison had his own can of soda. He didn't think his teeth could get any worse so why not indulge.

The man slurped his drink and looked over at Desiree, who still had her face covered. He knew what was under there, which was why he was willing to pay the extra. Besides, the room was only 15 bucks an hour.

"That sounds good to me," he shook Garrison's hand, sealing the deal and Desiree's fate.

"Perfect," Garrison said as he walked towards the door. "I'll leave you two alone and let you enjoy your date." He started opening the door and the man grabbed him by the shoulder. It wasn't rough, but it was more than enough to get Garrison's blood pumping.

"Wait," the man said. He was shiny with sweat, the anticipation almost too much.

Garrison turned, trying to calm his temper and the urge to jam his cobbler's knife into this fat fuck's neck.

"Yes," he replied, a bit of venom on his tongue.

"Can I have her key?" the man asked, almost begging. His eyes looked like a Basset Hound as he pleaded.

Garrison looked a little confused but began fishing the key from his pocket. "Sure, but what for? I doubt you want to stick your cock in between a zipper." He handed it to the man, who held it in front of his face like it was a great treasure.

"Oh no, I'm not that stupid," he chuckled, disrupting the pools of sweat that had gathered in his massive pores. "No, sometimes I just like to hear them scream."

What a sick fuck,' Garrison thought. "Yeah, sure. Whatever floats your boat. I'll be back in an hour and remember, don't fuck up her face. Understand?"

The man nodded and ushered Garrison out.

Garrison hadn't even made it off the property when he heard the first screams.

THE ALPHA

Desiree had finally stopped crying. She lay on the bed in the fetal position. Her insides felt like they were on fire, and she dreaded moving, let alone walking back to the shanty. The man had walked outside to have a cigarette, but he told her he was done. She didn't know if she believed him because adults lie, but she prayed.

She didn't think she could go through that again, let alone right after. The lock on the door rattled and she held her breath. For the first time in a long time, she hoped it was Garrison. Yes, he was an abusive piece of shit, but he never touched her…down there. Ever.

Garrison walked in and with him came the smell of fast-food burgers. He closed the door behind him.

"You did good, kid," he said, walking over to the unoccupied bed. He sat down, the springs groaning from years of abuse.

Desiree didn't answer, even though her mouth was unzipped. She only whimpered and shed silent tears.

"Here, eat something. Get your strength back up for the walk home." He unwrapped a cheeseburger halfway down and waited for her to turn around.

Desiree was in agony; not only that, but full of shame. It was nothing new, this wasn't her first date, and it probably wouldn't be her last. She knew it was better to take his charity and eat, rather than piss him off and starve. She turned and winced at the deep stabbing pain in her gut.

"Thank you," she muttered, taking the burger from his hand. As much as she wanted to scream in his face and throw the burger at him, she knew better. One day she'd get her chance. The first bite was nearly painful with how good it tasted.

The grease, fat, cheese, meat, and bread were like a heavenly ambrosia. It almost made the whole ordeal worth it. Almost…but not quite. She finished it in a few bites, wanting to savor it, but just couldn't. Her can of warm soda was on the floor and she picked it up. The sweetness was too much for her taste buds, but she drank anyway.

Garrison sipped on a thick milkshake, forgoing the burger.

Desiree was thankful, because if she had to chew for him, there was no way she'd not be able to swallow.

"Well, we have the room for 4 hours, so take advantage of the time and rest." He kicked his disgusting shoes off and laid on the bed. The entire room stunk of unwashed feet and grime.

Desiree wasn't one to turn down a real bed, especially when she normally slept on cardboard and tattered blankets.

Garrison was asleep within seconds.

Desiree hugged her tear-soaked pillow and closed her eyes. She hoped she would dream of a better life without Mary or Garrison or the fucking zipper.

Soon, she fell into a deep sleep. Her dreams were of a better life, but they were also filled with vengeance.

***

Mary had been out longer than she'd expected, and it was

almost dark. She hoped Garrison was in a good mood, that Desiree's date had gone well, and he wouldn't take it out on her.

The shanty was lit, which meant he must be cooking something. Mary's stomach rumbled at the thought of food. She was able to snag a decent looking slice of pizza out of the garbage, but that was hardly enough to fill her. She double checked the zipper and the lock, making sure everything was secure, before entering her dumpy house.

Garrison had a pan of chili on his makeshift burner. The goo bubbled as it warmed up, chunks of meat and beans rolled over one another.

Desiree sat quietly on her pile of cardboard and blankets. She had a blank look in her eyes, and she stared into the void.

"It's about fucking time," Garrison spat, not taking his eyes off the chili.

Mary closed the door behind her. The Fall air was getting colder and crisper every day. Soon the brutal winter would set in, freezing everything.

She didn't answer, for obvious reasons, but dug into her pockets. She pulled out a handful of razors, some tubes of make-up and a couple of small jars of lotion.

Garrison looked at the meager offerings. He took a deep breath, tapped the spoon on the side of the pan and stared at Mary.

"This is it? You're out there all fucking day, doing God knows what and this is what you come back with?" He stood up and grabbed her by the shoulders. "You mean to fucking tell me, this is it? No cash, no wallet, no jewelry? Huh?" He slapped her in the face. The sound of flesh on flesh was loud in the small room.

Desiree scurried away as best as she could.

Mary looked at him with apologetic tears in her eyes and mumbled through the zipper.

"No, you're fucking holding out on me," Garrison began going through her pockets. "Huh, where's the rest? Are you back on fucking dope again? Selling that nasty cunt for a hit of heroin?" Garrison began pulling her thin jacket off. "Take this fucking rag off," he demanded, as he kept yanking on it.

Mary twisted, trying to get her arms out before her shoulders dislocated.

Garrison searched the jacket, finding nothing. His breathing was sharp and shallow and his eyes wide.

"Take the rest off," he said, stepping back to look at her.

Mary furrowed her brows, as if not quite understanding.

"You can't talk, but I sure as fuck know you can hear. Take your fucking clothes off, you greedy bitch. I know you're fucking hiding something and when I find it…" he let it hang in the air. There was no need for a real threat, she knew what he was capable of.

Mary started slowly taking her shoes off. Her feet smelled almost as bad as his, but he didn't care. His greed and rage were fueling him and nothing else in the world mattered.

"Faster or I'll start cutting," to emphasize his point, Garrison drew his cobbler's knife from his pocket. The razor edge on the small blade shone in the firelight.

Mary had felt that knife before and didn't want to feel it again. She stripped faster, yanking her shirt overhead. Her bare breasts were withered from malnutrition, and her nipples stiffened in the cold. She pulled her pants down. Her matted pubic hair covered any notion of her gender. Goosebumps rose on her skin as she rubbed her arms to try and warm herself. Mary glanced over at Desiree, who was staring at her.

'Yeah, take it all in, you little bitch. Your fate will be worse than this,' Mary thought.

Garrison checked her over, even making her spread her ass cheeks. Nothing. No more merchandise. With uncanny speed, he slapped her in the face. He hit the lock securing her zipper and stung his hand.

"Fuck!" he yelled, flexing his fingers.

Mary stumbled back, the blow causing her to see double. A thin line of blood ran down her face, where his strike had caused the hoop piercing to tear. She put her hand to her face, touching the trickle of blood.

"Get fucking dressed!" he kicked at her clothes. "Your dirty cunt is stinking up the place."

Mary dressed, watching Garrison go back to the chili, which was now burning. She couldn't wait to see the look on his face when he felt Brian's blade.

***

Garrison was enraged. Mary should've come back with much more than what she'd brought. Instead, it was a day wasted and for what? A few packs of razors and make up. Still, it was better than nothing.

Their dinner was over and there wasn't much else left to do besides sleep, not that Garrison was tired. The four hours of shut eye he grabbed at the motel had done wonders for him. He felt refreshed. It was crazy what a bed, even a shitty one, can do for a person.

Garrison curled up in his dingy blankets, willing sleep to come for him. Anything to take him away from this hellish reality. And maybe, just maybe, he'd dream about his son.

***

Mary fought the urge to sleep, as badly as she wanted to. This was it. Her only shot to take Garrison out, to get him out of her life for good. No, she'd stay awake. She only needed to make it another few hours. That was it.

She was almost certain Garrison was asleep, but she didn't know what time it was. Gently and quietly, she reached between her legs and pulled an old watch from her vagina. Brian insisted on her having it, so they could get their timing right.

The military boy in him had never really left. She was nervous about the strip search and was thankful Garrison didn't make her squat and cough.

Mary pulled her blanket over her head and hit the button to activate the back glow feature of the watch. It was 9:30 PM. A half hour, which was all she needed. A half an hour to be free of the monster on the blankets next to her.

The minutes ticked by slowly, like time was stuck in the mud. Finally, the watch reached the golden hour. It was now or never.

Ever so quietly, Mary pushed back her blanket. She stood, using the dim light of the streetlamp to guide her to the door. The lock wasn't really a lock, more like a latch found on a gate. She began to open the door, holding her breath when the old hinges squeaked.

Garrison didn't move, just lay there, with the sound of rhythmic breathing coming from his rotten mouth.

The alley was dark, but an even darker shape stood there; Brian.

Mary pushed the door open all the way, giving the man room to enter. It was now or never.

***

Mary was always nervous, Garrison knew. But, when she'd returned and he stripped her, she was quivering. Not a lot, but more than enough for him to notice.

In the back of his head, he always knew the day would come where she would make her move and try to kill him. He didn't blame her; he was a piece of shit and knew it. Unfortunately for her and whatever stooge she'd convinced to kill him, he was a smart man.

The nap at the motel earlier in the day had left him fully rested. He probably could've slept, but something was telling him to stay up just a little longer. Garrison was glad he listened to his inner self.

He heard the heavy footsteps of another man enter his home. This man wouldn't live to see another day. Garrison always kept his knife nearby, but that night he had it in his hand and unsheathed.

Another step closer.

Garrison's heart was racing. He clenched the handle of his knife tighter. This had to be perfect or else he was fucked. He was at a disadvantage to begin with, as he was still laying down. If he didn't time it right, he'd tip his hand and that was it.

Another step.

The man was next to him now. Any second he'd hear a shuffle, closing that last little bit, getting him to knife range.

The man shuffled and Garrison struck.

Garrison threw his blankets off as the man was crouching down to stab him. The look of shock on his face was priceless, but Garrison couldn't relish in it too long. He had killing to do.

He slashed at the man's arm, the one holding the knife; a Ka-Bar by the looks of it. Garrison's slice was true, cutting his attacker's brachial artery.

"Fuck!" the man yelled. His knife went clattering to the ground as blood poured from his damaged arm. He stumbled back, trying to get away, but he would have no such luck.

Garrison was on his feet now and rushing the man. The look of fear in his eyes was what fueled Garrison. He reached up and grabbed the man's hair. There was no speech, no pomp and circumstance, just fucking violence. Garrison drove his blade under the man's jaw, hot blood ran down his hand. Again, he stabbed, seeking new flesh to destroy.

The man collapsed, but Garrison followed him to the ground. He set upon him like the predator he was, stabbing, stabbing.

Bubbles of blood popped from the man's mouth and

ruined throat, but Garrison didn't stop. He wanted to make a point.

Mary stood frozen; her zippered face locked in fear.

Desiree screamed through her zipper as she tried to push herself away from the two men on the floor. Blood was pooling on her pants, but she paid it no mind.

Finally, it was done. The man lay dead, with his throat opened wide. His shredded windpipe glistened in the dull light. Sliced tendons and destroyed blood vessels wept crimson as his heart shuddered for the last time.

Garrison stood, covered in blood. He looked like a maniac and for good reason.

Mary was shaking her head, her hands in front of her, as if saying she had no part of this.

Garrison approached her, the blade still in his hand. He looked down at it, tempted to jam it in her gut. No, he had a better idea for the traitorous bitch.

Mary lost control of her bladder, her pants darkening with strong urine. She collapsed, knowing she was dead.

Garrison wiped his blade on his pants and re-sheathed it. He grabbed Mary by her hair.

The woman moaned but didn't fight. She knew it was pointless.

"You tried to fucking kill me?" Garrison spat, almost nose to nose with her now. "You must be fucking stupid," he said, dragging her towards his blankets. He threw her down and began to rummage through his belongings. He pulled out a few pieces of thin wire.

"I knew you were fucking stupid, but even I can't believe you would try something so fucking insane." Garrison grabbed her wrists, put them behind her back and wrapped the wire around them.

Mary tried explaining herself through her zipper, but her jumbled pleas were unheard, nor cared for.

"Get the fuck up!" Garrison yelled.

Mary's wrists were starting to bleed, and she tried to plea more.

Garrison had no desire to listen to her whining. He kicked her in the legs.

"You have nothing left to say. Get the fuck up."

Mary slowly rose, instantly wishing that her hands were out in front of her.

"Outside, now," Garrison pushed Mary towards the

door. He heard a whimper in the corner; Desiree, almost forgotten about. "You too. Get up."

Desiree stood, her legs shaking as bad as Mary's. She tried not to look at the dead man at her feet, but it was difficult.

"Tonight, you're gonna learn what happens to people who cross me." He turned to Mary, "Get outside and start walking to the park."

Mary took a step into the darkness of the alley. For a moment she thought about running, but she knew it was no use. She was bound up and it was pitch black.

She could potentially make a dash for Brian's, but that was a long run in the dark when you were essentially blind. Her chance had passed when Garrison stepped up behind her and grabbed her hair.

Garrison put his bloody face against her ear. "Now, you're gonna find out what fucking pain is." He pulled her head back. "It will not be quick, nor easy, that I can guarantee you." His breath was rank and sour, but he didn't care. In fact, he kind of liked it. "Now let's go." He pushed her forward.

Desiree was frozen and couldn't find her legs. She didn't think she wanted to see what was going to happen to Mary, as much as she hated the woman.

"Hey, what are you doing?" Garrison looked back at her, realizing she wasn't with them. "Get your ass moving! You gonna learn what happens when someone tries to fuck with me."

Desiree became unfrozen. She looked in the opposite direction, the call of freedom almost overpowering her.

"Don't even fucking think about it," Garrison growled. He pushed Mary forward but looked back at Desiree. "If you think things are rough now, just wait 'til I catch you." He twisted the wire around Mary's wrists, eliciting a yelp from the woman. "This bitch is gonna find out," his lips were against her cheek. The zipper was inches from his mouth as he whispered. "Oh, I have something mighty nasty in store for you." He licked the dimpled skin and metal, relishing the taste of tears on her face.

Garrison picked up the pace, giving a back-glance to make sure Desiree was in tow. He knew she was, but he had to know for himself.

The night was quiet and became quieter when they reached the wood line where Garrison would trap strays. The full moon provided enough light to help them navigate their way through the trees, towards the old baseball field.

The sound of dogs barking could be heard in the distance. They walked past the field and the collection bin where that rich bitch had died months ago. No, they were heading somewhere else.

Tenke's junkyard had been closed for a few years, but it was still inhabited. Stray dogs had made it their little kingdom, slipping in and out from a hole in the fence, to live amongst the husks of old cars.

The mutts would roam the woods, hunting for whatever they could get their little mouths on; rats, raccoons, cats…people. There were stories of the dogs attacking people cutting through the woods or getting too close to the junkyard. Well, Garrison hoped the little fuckers were hungry.

"Push it open," he told Desiree, as they stopped outside of a rusted piece of fence.

The girl was shaking. The night wasn't cold, but she wasn't dumb. Something bad was about to happen. Something really bad.

Desiree pulled on the fence, careful to not cut herself on the rusted steel. On the streets, there were no doctors. Not that Garrison would let her go anyway. The zipper would be pretty difficult to explain, that was for sure. She peeled the section of the fence open, her little arms quivering to hold it.

"Walk," Garrison pushed Mary forward.

She didn't have a chance to duck. A piece of the fence caught her forehead, slicing her to the bone. Mary winced as hot blood ran down her face, into her eyes. The night air was chill against her exposed flesh and warm blood.

Garrison followed her through. "Come on," he said to Desiree, who was still fighting to hold the fence open. He didn't hold it for her.

Desiree maneuvered her way through the slit. The metal plucked at her clothes as she made her way. Thin scratches burned her skin, but nothing felt deep.

The junkyard was exactly that. Stacks of old cars stood quiet in the night. Broken glass was strewn over every inch of the ground and glittered like a million stars. Tires, random parts and even more cars were pillars to the old car gods. Nature had begun its reclaiming of the area with many of the cars sprouting weeds and even a few small trees. There were other things in the night…living things.

In the shadows of the junk, they moved. The dogs.

Mary began breathing heavy, her eyes darting from shadow to shadow.

Garrison kept his back close to the fence, but still drew his cobbler's knife. If any mangy fucks made a play for him, they'd regret it. Besides, they were about to get an easy meal.

Desiree looked around. She was calm as a long shadow moved from car to car. She couldn't place it, but the smell of animal waste and filth was relieving to her. Desiree took a deep breath, almost tasting the urea in the air.

Mary was far from calm. Her instincts were kicking in and she found her will to fight. Throughout her time on the streets, terrible things had happened to her; rape, sodomy, beatings and numerous overdoses. Nothing was as bad as her dog bite.

It wasn't long after she'd been on the streets, when Mary was bit by a stray. It wasn't much, just the wrong place at the wrong time, but it was more than enough to stick in her memory. That bite was electric and crushing. The feeling of teeth ripping into her flesh, violating her body, was enough to make her shudder. Then came the infection. People like to boast how dogs have cleaner mouths than humans. Well, that's a fucking lie. Mary's arm became hot with infection, weeping clear and yellow pus from the punctures. She thought she was going to die when the fevers started, but her body rallied and fought it off. Not this time though. There would be no death from infection, only violence.

Garrison whistled, trying to get the attention of the dogs. "Here, pups," he said, as if they could understand English. "Got some fresh skank for you," he whistled again.

Mary thrashed, kicking back towards his crotch. Her heel hit his thigh, not his balls like she'd intended.

"Fucking whore," Garrison said through gritted teeth. He cracked her in the temple with the handle of the knife.

Mary's world lit up like a camera flash and her knees felt like rubber. She was falling and didn't think Garrison could, or would, hold her up. She hit the packed earth, feeling a few small slices from the shattered glass.

"Oh, you wanna play fucking games, do you?" Garrison rolled her onto her stomach and sat on her bound hands.

Mary cried out through the zipper, little puffs of dust rising through the slits in the metal. Nausea was rising from the blow to the head, and she feared she'd vomit. She kept control of her gorge. A small fucking blessing.

"OK, here's a little game I like to call 'I'll never walk again,'" Garrison said. He grabbed Mary's left leg and sliced. Garrison wasn't a dumb man and in his many years, he learned how to hobble someone. Yes, a slice to the thigh or calf would hurt like a bitch, but that would heal. Now, popping those sweet, sweet tendons behind the knees, that was another story.

The cobbler's knife made short work of the tendons. They released like rubber bands under the steel of the blade. Blood began pouring from the laceration, staining Mary's dingy jeans. Her blood was dark in the moonlight and there was about to be more of it.

Mary screamed through the zipper. It was as if she were shouting into a pillow with a mouthful of broken glass. She thrashed and tried to kick, but her leg wouldn't cooperate.

Gore bubbled from her ruined flesh as her good leg tried to kick Garrison away. It was in vain.

"Ok, here comes number two," Garrison said, trying to get a hold on the flailing appendage.

Mary bucked, driving bits of glass deeper into her skin. She didn't care, she only knew if she didn't get away and fast, she'd never walk again.

"Fucking stay still," Garrison protested, fighting for the other leg. It was no use, she was giving it all she had. "Ok, I like the hard way."

Mary knew what was coming was going to be bad, she just didn't know how bad.

Garrison aimed the knife for her vagina and plunged it in. The blade didn't quite find her womanhood, like he'd intended, but made a much worse incision. The knife dug deep into her flesh, skipping off bone, as it sliced through the small patch of skin between her asshole and pussy. Some people call it the taint, but Garrison called it the sweet spot. He cut, sawing into her. More piss and blood poured from Mary's junkyard episiotomy. The fight was almost out of her.

With her leg still, Garrison grabbed it and cut. Again, the tendons popped free, the feeling vibrated his knife.

Mary's throat was raw. She cried and cried, the taste of blood in her throat. She didn't think it was possible to scream until you bled, but she'd proven that wrong.

Garrison was panting, like an animal. For a moment, he almost forgot why he was in the junkyard. A low growl brought him back to reality.

Six dogs emerged from the shadows, each one a mutt and battle-tested. The leader, a mud-colored mix breed with one ear, looked at Garrison. It growled, pulling its lips back to reveal a set of yellowed teeth.

"Easy, pup," Garrison spoke low. "Here's a nice juicy bitch for you," his hands were in front of him, the blade at the ready. He was questioning his decision of coming to the junkyard, when the rest of the eyes turned to him too.

Slowly, he walked backwards towards the hole in the fence. He hoped that dumb girl would have the wherewithal to open it for him, but he wasn't counting on it.

Mary groaned, sealing her death warrant. She wiggled, trying to get her face out of the glass. Fire burned in her crotch and legs.

A little dog, no bigger than a Jack Russell, sniffed at Mary's face. The thin crust of blood from the cut at the fence was mostly dry, but more than enough to entice the dog. It began licking at her, lapping hard to get the dry blood up.

Mary whined and moved her head. It was difficult on her stomach, but she did what she could.

The alpha dog gave Garrison a final glance and went over to inspect the woman.

The little dog nipped Mary's nose, tiny teeth drawing more blood.

She thrashed as hard as she could, but with no use of her legs and her genitals shredded, she couldn't do much.

The little dog bit her nose. Not a nip or a play bite. A full bite. The small mouth was latched firmly over Mary's nose.

Mary's bone and cartilage crunched under the jaws of the little beast. The dog ripped and thrashed, until the morsel of flesh and blood came free.

The zipper sealing shut Mary's mouth strained as she stressed her entire frame and attempted to scream. Angry welts of blood formed at the site of the cruel stitching, but Garrison's sewing skills held fast.

The fresh blood and screams were more than enough to set the other dogs in motion. The alpha decided it was time. The mangy dog moved in, targeting the streaming bloody crease between Mary's legs. The aggressive dog made short work of the denim, seeking out the soft, bloody meat underneath.

Mary flailed her useless legs as hellish jaws ripped her labia free.

The dog chewed her lips and pants as one, swallowing before setting back in for more. The rest of the beasts, seeing their leader enjoying prime parts, set on Mary.

It all became of blur of fur, meat and blood. The dogs ripped into her soft flesh, some of them choosing to tear apart her back, seeking organ meat. Others focused on the neck, knowing deep down this was the source of a lot of hot blood. The rest just bit what they could.

Garrison watched from the other side of the fence. He was intrigued, yet horrified. The dogs were truly savages. Much worse than any human being, at least he thought so. The screams and fighting had finally stopped, but Garrison could see the errant blood bubble rise from Mary's wounded throat.

He couldn't believe she was still holding on. Something else caught his attention; Desiree. The dumb little girl sat there, watching. Not a drop of fear or terror on her face. Well, Garrison couldn't have his prized money maker killed by dogs. No, she was still useful to him, at least for the time being.

"Desiree," he called to her. She either ignored him or couldn't hear over the yips and sounds of flesh tearing. "Hey, Desiree, let's go."

Desiree could hear him, yet she had no desire to answer him. At that moment, she knew she was done with Garrison. Whether her next decision led to her death or not, it didn't matter. Slowly, she looked towards Garrison, who had his hand on the fence, ready to open it for her. She looked away from him and into the gloom of the junkyard…and ran.

"Desiree," Garrison growled through gritted teeth. "Get the fuck back here."

The dogs saw a running meal. Some of them, the alpha included, gave chase.

Garrison watched them take off after her, into the night. She was as good as dead. He let go of the fence and walked away.

***

Desiree could hear the sounds of a dozen paws chasing after her. Her heart raced and she breathed through her nose as hard as she could. This suddenly didn't seem like a great idea anymore. A wall of cars and weeds seemingly rose out of nowhere, blocking her escape. She stopped and turned, watching the three dogs catch up to her.

A big one, the alpha, was dripping with blood. Its fat tongue hung from its mouth, little drops of blood mixed with saliva fell onto the dirt. There was something else. The dog had something in its mouth.

In the dim moonlight, Desiree couldn't tell what the dog was holding, but she had an idea.

The alpha approached Desiree until it was only inches from her. It looked at her with battle-worn eyes and opened its mouth. An unidentifiable chunk of meat fell from its jaws, landing on Desiree's shoes.

She didn't want to take her eyes off the big dog, but she had to. Desiree broke eye contact and looked down.

The alpha moved.

***

Garrison was nearly out of the wood line when he heard the howls. It sounded like Desiree didn't make it too far.

FEELING FESTIVE

October. This was Garrison's favorite time of the year. Not only did it bring back a hearty dose of nostalgia, but the weather was pretty damn nice. Garrison always loved the Fall, ever since he'd been little. It was his favorite time of the year, with the best weather, best colors, and of course, Halloween. When Tyler was born, he was ecstatic to go Trick or Treating again. Hell, he even dressed up himself, a few times. Things had changed.

He still loved the Fall, but bitter memories of a little hand clenched in his, cut him. It roiled in his gut like sour milk. His costume was now a permanent one; a fucking bum. It was authentic all right, with stained, ripped and disgusting clothing. His skin had the perfect shade of grime, and his patchy beard was disheveled and matted. His few remaining teeth completed his look, with their blackness and bloody gumline. Yup, great fucking costume indeed.

It could get cold at night, but that wasn't much of an issue. The animals were plentiful and moving, trying to stock up for the winter. This made them much easier to trap, giving him a good supply of meat.

He'd become pretty handy in the canning department and routinely canned cat, squirrel, dog or whatever other meat he could.

It had been a few months since the night in the junkyard. Things hadn't been better for Garrison, but they were far from worse. Many people wouldn't give handouts to a single guy, so the begging front was suffering. Although, with the holidays approaching, people were a bit more generous, even if he was a single male.

Garrison was taking a nap on his pile of filthy blankets. His day had been decent, with a few quarters found at the laundromat, a couple bucks from begging and even a can of dog food stolen from a bodega. It wasn't his favorite meal, but he was hungry. If there was anything in his snares, he'd add it to the doggy chow and have a nice stew.

He awoke to the gloom of the streetlight filtering through the tarps. A cool, October breeze ruffled the coverings, letting in the smell of garbage and dead leaves.

Garrison rubbed his face, which was perpetually covered with patchy stubble. His stomach growled and he considered heating up the dog food then and there, and forgoing the traps. No, he couldn't do that. This time of the year the traps had to be checked daily. If not, any catch would be scavenger food before the morning. Not to mention, the meat would rot, and Garrison couldn't afford to get sick again. A few months prior, he'd eaten a questionable opossum and ended up shitting and puking for three days straight. This was rough in a house with running water and creature comforts, like a bed, but it was a filthy agony living on the streets.

Garrison grabbed his few supplies; a flashlight, a plastic bag, and of course, his knife. He tucked everything into his coat and headed out. He couldn't wait to see what was waiting for him.

The city was in full Halloween mode, with the holiday only days away. Buildings were decorated with ghoulish images. Pumpkins and Jack-'o-Lanterns adorned steps.

Even the public works got involved, hanging orange and black banners from the street lights. Garrison's mind drifted back to happier times, times he tried to keep from his thoughts, times with his son.

The streetlights cast pools of light, dispelling some of the shadow, but not all. Garrison lived in those shadows, no, he lurked in those patches of blackness.

He found himself on the outskirts of the city, the trees of his hunting area not far away.

"I hope I got one of them little fuckers tonight," he said to himself as he began navigating the dark woods.

"AHHHHHHHHH! HELP ME! SO-SOMEBODY FUCKING HELP ME!" A voice screamed, piercing the night air.

Garrison listened, trying to pinpoint where the sound was coming from, then he figured it out.

The old baseball field. The clothing collection bin.

"Could it be?" he asked himself aloud, peering into the gloom of the forest. His eyes couldn't see more than a few feet, but he was certain where the sound was coming from. Garrison moved into the trees with purpose, taking the trails like an expert. He didn't quite run for fear of tripping, but he was far from walking.

'I hope this little fucker is good and stuck and has a fat wallet,' he thought, as he brushed an errant branch from hitting him in the face. *'I could use a good payday, that's for sure.'* Garrison was starting to breathe heavy. Partially from the unfamiliar physical exertion, and partially from the thought of some cold, hard cash.

The clearing was in sight and sure as shit, Garrison could see someone dangling from the bin. The same bin he left that rich bitch to die in.

This time it was a teenage boy hanging from the bin with a knocked over garbage can next to his feet. The boy was quiet, a steady stream of blood dripping from his mangled arm. Garrison approached cautiously; his dirty fingers wrapped around his blade.

"Eh," Garrison said, getting closer to the boy. He was still breathing, but barely. "You still with me, buddy?" Garrison asked as he nudged the boy's leg with his boot.

The boy moaned but offered no resistance. Garrison smiled, his black teeth reflecting the moonlight.

"Jackpot," Garrison began rifling through the boy's pants, pulling out a wallet. He opened it quickly, just to see if it was worth it. Most kids didn't carry much cash, but something was better than nothing. A couple of bills peeked up at him. His smile, like that of a rotten Jack-o'-lantern, widened to comical proportions. He'd gotten his treat and the trick was pulling in with its headlights off.

"Hey! What's going on here?" a voice said from the shadow.

Garrison turned, shocked that he didn't hear a car pull up. A spotlight and overhead police lights lit up the night to near daylight.

"Oh fuck," Garrison moaned. He didn't want to get arrested, that was certain. He looked around, seeking an escape. He couldn't run towards the woods, which was almost right at the cop. Besides, he didn't think he could make it through the woods in a full sprint and once the cop called for backup, he was toast.

"What are you doing to that boy?" the cop asked. He had his flashlight out and trained on Garrison.

Garrison's heart was racing. He heard the cop key up his radio and mumble something. The cavalry was on the way and he needed to get the fuck out.

"Don't you fucking move," the cop ordered, and Garrison could hear the sound of a gun being drawn.

'Fuck this,' Garrison thought. He didn't think the cop would shoot him, especially with a wounded kid hanging up. He decided to chance it and ran.

"Hey, stop!" the cop yelled. He did a double take at the boy and the extent of his injuries. Even though he wanted to chase Garrison, the cop didn't.

Garrison ran and ran hard. His old, battered lungs

burned, but every step brought him farther from the red and white emergency lights and closer to freedom.

A massive chain link fence stood in front of him, and he dug around for the cut. His fingers pried the fence apart and he slipped into the confines of the junkyard. Déjà vu hit him and he thought about Mary and the night she had tried to have him killed. She'd learned the hard way not to fuck with him. In fact, he was standing in almost the exact same spot where the dogs ripped her apart. He grinned, knowing her last moments were fucking agony.

"He went this way," a voice said, approaching the fence.

Garrison saw a pair of cops, the backup units, running. Their flashlights bobbed in the darkness as they searched for him. Garrison didn't want to go deeper into the junkyard, but he had no choice.

The pillars of cars popped up all around him and soon, he was disoriented.

'Was this how Desiree felt when she ran away?' he thought, trying to find a way out of the maze of steel and rubber. His legs were shaking. The adrenaline of finding the kid and running from the cops was catching up to him. He leaned against an old Ford and rested. Garrison never saw Desiree watching him, but she sure as shit saw him.

***

The night was quiet until the boy started screaming. Desiree and her pack were contemplating checking on the boy but thought against it. Nothing good could come from him and in the end, she decided to stay put. Then, she heard the chase. Someone was coming towards her yard, her territory. As soon as she heard the fence being peeled back, she knew she was in for a wild night. She couldn't have imagined it being Garrison, the bane of her existence.

Seeing Garrison enter the junkyard brought back a flood of memories, the most prominent one on her face. She reached up and touched her lip-less smile. The zipper wasn't easy to cut off and she took more meat than metal, but it was no longer a part of her. Desiree's lips were gone, and her teeth were permanently exposed, but she could talk, growl and even smile, if needed.

She smiled a crooked, misshapen smile, watching Garrison run deeper into the junkyard. His fate was sealed, he just didn't know it yet. Desiree stalked him from the shadows, the dogs only a few steps behind her. For years she was tormented by him, used by him and now it was his turn to feel pain and fear.

Garrison leaned against an old Ford and Desiree could hear him breathing heavy. It was time.

Desiree slid underneath the car, her makeshift glass knife in hand. It wasn't much, but she didn't have much use for a blade. All her meat was raw and ripped apart with her teeth. Ever since the day she was offered a chunk of Mary's flesh, she hadn't had use for cooked meat. The more blood, the better.

Garrison's Achilles tendons were taut as he leaned against the car.

Desiree could see the tops of the tendon peeking out from Garrison's boots. She slithered closer, almost in range. Finally, she was there. Desiree's heart was racing. This was her chance and probably her only chance to get redemption. She wasn't going to mess it up. Desiree gripped the knife tight and sliced. The glass made short work of socks and flesh. Both tendons were cut clean and deep.

"AH!" Garrison screamed. He took a stumble-step forward and his tendons peeled away from their muscle in a wet rip. Blood began to flow as he fell face first into the packed earth.

"Sucks, doesn't it," Desiree said as she crawled out from underneath the car, the glass knife still in her hand.

Garrison rolled over; the familiar voice worked its way through the pain.

"You little fucking cunt," he spat when he saw Desiree

standing over him, his blood wetting the edge of her knife. "I'll fucking gut you. I'll cut you from your little snatch all the way to your fucking throat." He pulled his knife from his pocket. Garrison braced himself and tried to stand. "Ah, fuck!" he groaned, the severed tendons reminding him of his injury.

Desiree grinned. It still felt odd without the zipper and with her mangled lips, but it was a good kind of odd.

"No, I think your days of cutting are over," as if on command, the dogs surrounded her.

They were slunk low and had their ears back. Since the last time Garrison had been in the junkyard, the pack had grown. Some new and hungry faces were watching the bleeding man like a snack.

Garrison backpedaled. He screamed and left streaks of gore with each thrust.

"No, leave me the fuck alone," Garrison waved his knife at the approaching dogs. "I'll fucking kill you mutts, I fucking swear it!" His eyes were wide, and spittle flew from his rotten mouth. The pack began closing in, nipping at his bloody feet. "Fuckers!" Garrison swung the knife at the dogs but couldn't yet reach them. He kicked, hitting a dog in the snout. The shock caused his destroyed tendons to flair in pain, but it kept the dogs back. He never saw the alpha, the massive, mangy stray, moving in behind him.

Desiree did all she could to contain herself and not look at the big dog, but her glee finally gave way.

Garrison saw the gleam in her eyes and dared look away from the pack.

The jaws of the dog snapped out, like a viper's strike, and closed around his wrist. Numbing, shattering and crushing pain, brought Garrison's focus to razor sharp. Time seemed to slow down as his arm snapped. Each pop of bone was felt in detail. Each puncture from every single yellow tooth, burned his flesh. His fingers had a life of their own, springing open and dropping his beloved knife to the ground.

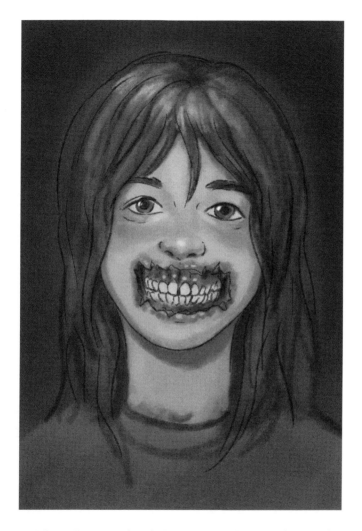

The pain was red and electric, something he'd never felt before.

More was coming.

Garrison looked back towards Desiree and the pack of dogs. Another large one, this a bully-breed mix, lunged for his face.

The dog's short snout fit directly over Garrison's mouth. Hot, dog breath flooded his mouth, along with blood. The dog bit, using every ounce of strength to break Garrison's lower jaw, nearly removing it in one bite.

Garrison screamed into the dog's maw; a spray of blood followed his muted cries. He punched at the block head of the dog, but he might as well have been hitting wood.

The pack moved as one, each targeting a soft bit of flesh. One dog made its move right away, clamping its jaws around Garrison's cock and balls. The man screamed, but the big dog still had his face firmly in its jaws, crushing and ripping. Garrison's manhood was torn off in bloody strings of flesh and dirty denim. The dog retreated with the hairy, gory meat and ate. There wasn't much to enjoy.

Another dog, this one with a longer snout, started at his gut. The tight jaws made quick work of fabric and flesh as it burrowed its way into loops of intestines. The smell of human shit and torn stomach cavity filled the cool, Fall air. It was the smell of a feast for the dogs. Black shit and green slime covered the dog's muzzle, but it lapped up the filth like a fine meal.

Garrison was bit, chewed and eaten. His blood quenched dry earth and thirsty mouths. His dead eyes stared at the moon and every twinkling star in the sky.

The dogs ripped, fought and growled as they tore Garrison to pieces. All under the watchful eye of Desiree.

The young girl, the queen of her little kingdom of mutts, watched and smiled. Her ruined face was crooked and tattered, but with no zipper. In the dimness of the October night sky, Desiree sat smiling, looking like a rotting Jack-'o-lantern.

ABOUT THE AUTHOR

Aron Beauregard is an author of extreme horror, Splatterpunk, and a purveyor of escargot. His love of snails started at a young age, and he hasn't looked back. He pardons one snail a year and his current pet snail is named Carl. Aron and Carl live happily in a Ford Windstar

ABOUT THE AUTHOR

Daniel J. Volpe is an author of extreme horror, Splatterpunk, and the president of the Jort Alliance of America (or the JAA). His deepest passions are keeping his abnormally hairy legs exposed, never straying from his denim demon roots, and keeping dads everywhere connected. Aside from experimenting with the finest hotel sausage gravy that can be found across the country, of course.

Made in the USA
Las Vegas, NV
22 November 2024

12402091R00092